Dreamers of Dreams

Sidney Mttron Hirsch

Dreamers of Dreams

Rex E. Wiederanders

Illustrated by Gavin Davies

Walnark Publishing
Tucson, AZ

Walnark Publishing
6890 E Sunrise Drive #120-227
Tucson, AZ 85750-0840

ISBN: 0-9740497-0-0
Cover art and text illustrations: Gavin Davies
Design and typesetting: Carol Delattre

Library of Congress Control Number: 2003104784

2 3 4 5 6 7 8 9 10

Manufactured in the United States of America
Post Litho Printing
1122 N. Stone Ave.
Tucson, AZ

To Sidney Mttron Hirsch,
master teacher and eternal friend.

To the Carole in my heart.

This is a work of fiction;
only the dreams are real.

Preface

I met Mr. Hirsch when he was quite old but still looked and acted like a young man. I was an Air Force physician at Sewart Air Force Base in Smyrna, Tennessee and very unhappy about it. A patient whose family had befriended me took this quite seriously and insisted I meet a "most unusual old man." At first I resisted but her extraordinary persistence changed my mind and she drove me to Mr. Hirsch's little house on Acklen avenue in Nashville. As we inched up the long dirt drive, I saw him standing on the back porch, illuminated by a bare light bulb. He appeared rooted into the very head of God and I was swept by an overwhelming feeling of peace. All my irritations fled: I had come home. When we reached him I got out of the car and stepped up on the porch. He took my hand, shook it, and almost broke it. This man was destined to be the friend of my life. As a physician I have met many bright people—compared to all and any of them he was extraordinary. The only way to understand his power was to be in his presence.

I decided to take a surgical residency in Vanderbilt so I could study with him. For the next five years we met once a week, then I left to establish my private medical practice. He was my teacher and I was his only student. He was kind, gentle, always formal, and called me "Doctor." We met in his home in rooms filled with antiques, rare books, a vast library with many dictionaries, and a marble head of Buddha that smiled when light came from above and frowned when light came from below. He was always in command; I asked questions but he directed the study.

Mr. Hirsch was particularly interested in Greek, Sanskrit, and Hebrew, but also knew Latin, Egyptian, German, French and other languages. He studied the deep symbolic origins of language and the factors leading to the Western subconscious. On the night we met, he introduced me to a Greek word for pine tree, showing me a metaphor for the vertical human spine. This hooked me. I learned that dream symbols, word symbols, and symbol symbols are all the same—we comprehend the world because we are able to manipulate symbols and put them in their proper order: the brain is a symbol-handling device.

He drew from the Greek and Hebrew Bible, the Kabbalah, the Bhagavad-Gita, the Upanishads, and Egyptian and Zen Buddhist documents. He also referred to classic writers—Homer, Plato, Shakespeare, the Greek play-wrights, the Yellow Emperor, and to modern luminaries such as Carl Jung, Sigmund Freud, Walt Whitman, Herman Hesse, James Joyce, and Salvador Dali.

Mr. Hirsch never gossiped about his family or past. I learned a few things from his acquaintances and his sister, Goldie. As a young man he joined the Navy and became the lightweight boxing champion of the South Pacific. When discharged, he elected to leave ship at Yokohama and traveled throughout the Orient consulting religious leaders and masters; he knew Vivekananda quite well. He went to France, posed for Rodin, and visited Gertrude Stein. He then moved to New York and began a career as a playwright.

At age twenty-six he was struck by a debilitating ill-ness. He returned to Nashville to live with his sister and brother-in-law James Marshall Frank. His script "The Fire Regained" was used for a production in Centennial Park. On Sunday afternoons, the Frank home was open to Vanderbilt students. Propped up on a lounge chair he began to meet regularly with the group he named the Fugitives. They published nineteen editions of the poetic magazine, *The Fugitive*, between April, 1922 and December, 1925. The publication closed for a most unusual reason—it became so successful that no one could handle it.

Preface

The Fugitives had "formed the major school of 20th Century poetry in America."[1]

Several of the group became highly acclaimed. The novelist Robert Penn Warren won three Pulitzer Prizes and was the country's first Poet Laureate. William Y. Elliot became head of the department of government at Harvard and counselor to six presidents. John Crowe Ransom founded *The Kenyon Review* and, along with Allen Tate, Donald Davidson, and Robert Penn Warren, became a leader of the Agrarian movement. Merrill Moore, a noted psychologist, dubbed Mr. Hirsch "the guiding light" behind the founding of the group.

Mr. Hirsch recovered from his illness at age thirty-three and retreated to self-directed study. His reclusive life was punctuated by a few legendary events. Three weeks before World War II began he had worked out the starting date. He gave this to Captain Walter Jones who commanded President Roosevelt's yacht and asked him to put it on the president's desk. The day the war started Mr. Hirsch received a call from Roosevelt inviting him to Washington. He spent the war years there as advisor to the president on European and Far Eastern affairs. When the war ended, he returned to Nashville. I like to think of him as a "sleeping dragon." This was said about Chinese scholars of high rank who left the royal court and pursued the flaming pearl. Having gotten it, the sleeping dragons waited until the court woke them to their further responsibilities.

Dreamers of Dreams gives the essence of Mr. Hirsch as I recall him. The kind and gentle Dr. Zvee is thus the two of us but weighs most heavily on him. The dreams and dialogue are loosely presented to show interplay between the subconscious and the conscious mind. Dream study and the probing of dream meanings is at best an uncertain and vast science and might be taken with a spoonful of courage; humor is even more important. So step inside and meet Dr. Zvee.

Preface

I thank B. Leah Sheeler and Samantha Nelson for their excellent contributions to the manuscript, Corinne Davies for encouragement and editorial help that made the book possible, and Carol Delattre for detailed editorial comments and book design.

Rex Wiederanders
April 1, 2003

[1]William Pratt, *The Fugitive Poets: Modern Southern Poetry in Perspective*. J.S. Sanders and Company, Nashville TN, 1991.

the first meeting

Dreams are like virtues,
they always give more than they promise.

"You do yourself and your dreams, and all dreams, a great disservice. Dreams are very important."

"But I thought dreams were just, well, illusions, figments of the imagination, nothing at all substantial, as I've heard my mother say often enough."

"That is the usual feeling toward them. But do you really think such minds as Jung and Freud would have been so interested in them if they had been only illusion? Especially Dr. Jung. He was a great master of the dream. They both understood that the dream throws light on areas that are otherwise quite obscure to us. Do you remember what Plato said about them?"

"I didn't know he spoke of dreams."

"Oh, yes, Mrs. Darnely." Dr. Zvee's eyes twinkled with the pleasure of introducing June to this delightful ancient man. "Dreams have always been extremely important to those who are reaching for the borders of learning. All these souls have looked about them, seen the beauty of art, heard the magic of music, wondered at the immense literature built up by mankind and tried to find that vibrant source from whence they all spring. The wise ones have always known that man is not creative and yet some of these dreams are things of sublime creativity. So there must be a realm that gives birth to all this beauty—there is and it has many names. If you ask for directions you will be sent to the Pure Land or to *Das Ferne Land* or to the Land of Havillah where there is gold and the gold of that land is good. Beauty is there and there we must go to find her. And if our dreams are true and if they guide us in the truth we shall get there, indeed.

He continued, "Plato alludes to this place in many of his works and details our connections to it. He tells of two gates that open to send celestial information: one of ivory and the other of horn. It is from these that dreams emerge. Imagine that! Dreams are the connecting link to creativity. I was surprised to read that the prophetic or true dreams come from the gate of horn. It seems that they, being more valuable, should come from that which is more valuable, the ivory. Until I really thought about it. Then I realized that horn is compacted hair and hair being long is the very symbol of longing. So horn is compacted longing and horns are grown according to the infinite plan of the logarithmic life spiral."

He smiled as he saw the frown of concentration about her eyes. "It does seem that the further one goes the more complex it becomes. We do have to know about logarithmic spirals and other exotics to interpret our dreams. As of this moment just remember that horns are the very symbol of life. That is why Salvador Dali made such a fuss about them. You may not remember this incident but he was at the Louvre and doing a copy of *The Lacemaker* by Vermeer, when he produced a picture of the rhinoceros' horn instead. He saw those life spirals in Vermeer's work.

Can you follow any of this?"

"It 's not particularly easy."

"We will go over it, perhaps more than you wish, for this is very important to your understanding. When you do begin to really understand, it will be quite apparent where the fairy tales, epic poems, hero legends and mystic adventure stories originated. They were dreams as dreamed by dreamers of dreams and they were told and retold until mankind grew up and they could be written down on the rock anchors of our heritage. Each one is a scene or even a complete play acted out in accordance with its own plot but containing in its seed the proper answers to the life questions of that moment. How the Angels of Dreams who send these illuminations must sort and sift among their myriad stores, taking them up like fine jewels until the perfect one is found. And then they hurl the fragile shaft of light that splashes its new reality on the altar of our minds. Their azure wishes for our comprehension of their gift come along as a footnote. I can see them clustering together, thinking the intense thoughts that aim to pierce the dark heart of our understanding. And yet, laughing gently at our steps that go astray—unless the sickness of soul is upon us. Then from their vast vocabulary of images and ideas they compound their tinctures and balsams and lay them like tender dressings on our minds, renewing and reviewing until the healing is complete. Those who can read their images, the few who are privileged to interpret their dreams, may follow their therapy and watch while the Angels of Dreams like gentle midwives bring the evil forth within a healing light."

"You make them sound so mysterious! I had no idea there were Angels of Dreams. Do they really exist?"

He smiled, beaming wrinkles that crinkled at his eyes. "I would be very sad to learn one day that they do not really exist, for it does make a lovely story, does it not?"

"Oh, I love it!" Her voice caught in the pleasant

excitement. "But, if these Angels of Dreams go to all that trouble, what do these dreams do?"

"Before we answer that, let us go over dreams in general and then sort out the particular types we can recognize. Science does not make these distinctions with particular accuracy and I do think that is all to the good. It is not prudent to be too obvious in the dispensation of angelic information. Goethe said on this delicate point, 'We should only express those of the highest truths, which will be to the good of the world. The rest we must keep to ourselves: like the soft rays of a hidden sun, they will shed their light upon all our actions.' Do you follow this?"

"Yes, I follow it. Does that mean we can't discuss these things?"

"No, no, not at all. In this room when we speak together privately, everything may be discussed. Frankness is our mode, Mrs. Darnely, that you not lose your way on the path in this miasma of nebulosity. Are you ready?"

She nodded and smiled. "O.K. I'm ready."

"Then, dreams are our subject. First we shall lay out their territory. What is it that makes them different from the thoughts and images that pattern our waking state? When we have answered this to your satisfaction, we will divide them into their types."

She nodded her agreement as his voice shifted into a slower, deeper professorial tone. "Dreams differ from our usual waking thoughts in several ways. First, all dreams are will driven. As you have free will and can soar in your imagination to envision many actions that your body awake could never do, so in dreams you may do whatever your will might suggest, though it would be death for your body to try it. Second, all dreams are played outside the four dimensions. That means the Angels of Dreams can juxtapose figures and beings and the laws of flow of images may proceed in any sequence they desire. Third, the dream takes place in the immediate

Now and is not concerned with the past. Some are revealing of the future but they do not dwell there. Fourth, dream light, or Now-Light as I prefer, follows the law of infinity, which does not have a single or particular source. Unless, of course, the dream is used as an excuse for the Angels of Dreams to place the dreamer into a real situation under a dream cover."

She drew her breath in sharply. "The first three points are bad enough, but that fourth point. Do you mean that some dreams are real? That they actually happen?"

"*Très difficile.*" He murmured several times, turning over various approaches that might be less shocking. "Yes, I do." He began slowly. "I strongly suspect some dreams are real and *actually happen.* When the dreamer meets herself, even if she does not die as is commonly believed, I think the self she meets is real. The yogis have studied this event at very great length. They meet the Atman. They meet the Ishvara. Both of these are real and reproducible phenomena. I also think some of the meetings with one's forbears are real." His voice dropped into a soft and confidential tone as though he wished not to be heard even by the spirits that could be around them. "I also suspect that the images seen by highly intelligent children when they wake in the deep night are real." He chuckled deep in his chest as he saw a chance to escape into comedy. "Does any of this strike you as humorous?"

"No." She said in surprise. "No, rather the opposite, with all this talk of dying and meeting some strange new things with strange new names in the deep night."

"Do not let them frighten you. It occurred to me that the disparity we find in our humor between free will and what it can envision, and the actions possible to our bodies, is a good and funny analog of our first point about dreams. In dreams, we see through our free will as we do in humor. Think of Calvin and Hobbes. All fanatic devotees of this comic strip will recognize Calvin's actions as driven by free will. He tells his parents off in raucous terms when he's alone with Hobbes but when he's with his mom he's properly respectful." They both laughed and the tension vanished.

Dr. Zvee continued. "Have we drawn a clear enough distinction between dreams and our waking thoughts?"

"I believe we could add one more distinction."

"What is that, Mrs. Darnely?"

"Dreams are totally incomprehensible. I simply can't make head or tail out of mine."

"Ah." He smiled. "That is an excellent point. Are they incomprehensible because they are meaningless or because we cannot read their language?"

"From the way you introduced dreams, I think I had better say it's because we can't read them."

"Wisely chosen. A dream is a medium, a pictorial rebus that is and is not meant for the waking mind. If all the information in each dream were given to us immediately we would bend under the load. Too much too soon! And that may be a mortal blow to the mind not yet hardened. So the dream conveys the information and the dreamer may take only as much as she can understand, which is tantamount to saying as much as her mental strength will bear. Consider Joseph and the dreams of Pharaoh. Do you not see that he and he alone was able to bear the information load of those dreams?" His voice rose. "Of all the souls in Egypt, only he, a prisoner and a sojourner and a stranger in that land, could bear the mass of that weight.

"Dreams are deeply obscure to the non-dream-tutored because they speak in the universal and stable language of symbol manipulation. This language is quite as precise as the language of mathematics and perhaps even more difficult to learn. So even though dreams are not . . . I can say it even more strongly, dreams are never untrue, but their presentation easily leads the unwary astray.

"I think we have said enough on this. Shall we proceed?" She nodded. "Then it is time to tell you of the types of dreams. There are three of these and they all follow the laws that distinguish them from waking thought. There is great overlap between them, for like all of life, these type differences are not starkly black nor white but their edges blur to gray. Nonetheless, if you understand these distinctions well, you should have a reasonably firm grasp on these vacuous ideas, and for you, dreams may bend to logic. Not understanding this distinction has led to much controversy and confusion in the business of dream analysis.

"The ones that cause the most emotional upset are the Type-1 dreams, the standard nightmares. These are but the acting out of sexual fantasies. You can distinguish them from others as they are filled with emotion, usually fear. There is a lot of falling off cliffs and running and waking up covered with sweat just before being eaten or caught or chopped into small pieces. These are all of that kind. They all have to do with one's fears of and desires for sex. This is a terrible subject for a small child and brings both pain and destruction until adulthood finally puts it in perspective. If you ever get to Switzerland be sure to see the paintings of Hodler. They are in most of the museums there. He shows this fear most powerfully and plainly and at least one of his pictures is titled *Nightmare*. These dreams are lynch pins for the psychiatrist because controlling sex with its immense power is exactly tantamount to controlling our lives. Another cause of nightmares that is not so well recorded is the visitation of young children by spirits and ghosts, real or imagined."

"Do you really think ghosts exist?"

"The burden of evidence says they do. Some children can actually see these for children are not as ghost-proof as we adults. No wonder they have such terrible night terrors. I wonder how many children have ruined their precious childhood time by these phantasms? And of course, telling them ghost stories at bedtime certainly does not help them sleep." His eyes crinkled into his noiseless laughter. "Have you ever considered what a hold terror has on us?"

She nodded and answered his smile. "I know the bookstores are jammed with every kind of horror tale one can imagine. Do you know why?"

"It might be that we need the awful sting of this terror to assure us of our own reality. Desperate therapy, I would say." They both shook their heads.

"Do these nightmares interest you?" she asked.

"No, not at all. Neither do the Type-2 dreams that are more usually called the Maintenance dreams. These are difficult to remember because of a flood of energy that bombards the cortical brain and renders it numb. Their outstanding feature is that they try to keep us asleep so they can do their work. We have all had those intense dreams in the morning when we are trying to out-shout the alarm to allow us a few more precious moments in that comfortable bed.

"Scientific investigation has shown we have two modes of sleep: deep sleep and REM or rapid eye movement sleep. Type-2 dreams keep pace to these rapid eye movements. In deep sleep, our bodies are quiet as are our minds but when REM sleep takes over, as it does every ninety minutes or so all night long, then we set ourselves to the solution of problems. Most of these have to do with the repetitively mundane jobs of our daily living. We map our physical territories, but far more important we also map our mental territories. Psychiatrists probe deeply into these dreams using many tricks to help their patients remember them. For they are very good signposts and benchmarks of our adaptation to daily life. You might say that these dreams reprogram our minds much as a computer is reprogrammed to upgrade its efficiency. We do not remember these dreams so it has been necessary for a lot of scientists to wake up a lot of experimental subjects to prove that these dreams truly do exist and to correlate them with wake-a-day activities. If you wish to record these maintenance dreams, keep a tablet and pen at your bedside and the moment you wake write out exactly what you have dreamed.

"Animals dream these REM dreams just as we do, especially territorial animals. They dream them and run while they are dreaming. It looks exceedingly droll to see a dog lying on his side sound asleep carrying out the violent motions of running. This is to imprint on the animals' minds the boundaries of the territory in which they live and where they find their living. These boundaries are vital to their survival. We humans have these as well."

"Then these dreams are very important."

"Oh, yes, extremely important. Nature rarely deals in the superfluous. Even if I have no ready explanation for nightmares, I suspect they also are necessary and important. But there is no doubt about Maintenance dreams. They are extremely important. I would re-quote Hamlet on this point. Instead of 'To sleep, perchance to dream.' I would say to sleep because we must dream. How long have we assumed that we sleep at night because there is no sunlight for our work? But there are animals that sleep during the light of day and hunt or work at night so we know now that we sleep when it is convenient for us. But we also know we must get in a certain minimum time at dreaming. If we are deprived of deep sleep we will get very sleepy and finally have to have an uninterrupted night but that is about all. If we are deprived of REM sleep, we can have some very severe symptoms of mental unbalance and we must dream until we have made up for what we have lost. Do you not see now that we sleep because we must dream?" Her doubtful expression showed him what she saw.

"No? Well, it is but a thought. But we can agree that both of these dream types are very important to our mental processes and their maintenance. Although," he mused into the space before him, "I must admit, all psychiatrists do not really understand the difference between all dreams. Would you believe that, Mrs. Darnely?" He chuckled again as she nodded in agreement. "Jung, however, makes no mistake. He has a lot of very important dreams in his reported work and he includes many Maintenance dreams but when he comes to Type-3 dreams, as he does in *Man and His Symbols,* he looks deeply into religion and philosophy. You may read the dreams of the little girl who presented them to her father as a Christmas gift and follow the intense efforts Jung makes to understand them." He fell silent for awhile.

"So the Type-3 is the third type with all that entails?" she offered.

"I have no better name for them so I call them Type-3 dreams. They are at least as important as the first two types as they are a strong support and the inspiration of our religions. This type follows the general description of dreams I have already given you but there are a few more qualities that set it apart. Type-3 dreams tend to be intensely personal. The dreamer usually does not confide these to anyone but her specific teacher or dream professional. She may wait years to find just the right person. In the meantime, no one else will even know of their existence. What prevents this I do not know. Do you know why you never shared your dreams before we met?"

"Well, for one thing, I really thought no none else would be interested. And I was sure I would be laughed at or made fun of if I talked about them. As you say, they are very personal. It would be like taking off my clothes before strangers or baring my soul and you do not do this until you find one who really understands."

"That is a moment of very great comfort."

"The great moment in our life."

"Indeed. Indeed. Indeed it is. But we should go on about our dreams. Perhaps the most important and most difficult aspect of these dreams is the language that encodes them. They are given in symbols and must be understood as symbols and they are the very fountain of symbols. Jung makes a great effort to distinguish symbols from signs. He says the sign is always less than the concept it represents while the symbol stands for more than its obvious and immediate meaning. The symbol is used to represent the things that are beyond the range of human understanding, like the soul and the mind and eternity. We can speak of these incomprehensible things in symbolic terms and very probably do so because these symbols were learned in dreams eons ago and written down. Thus, we may have some understanding of this language. The best synopsis I believe to have been written on symbolic language was done by Alfred Jarry. I found it in the paper that William Anastasi presented at the Sorbonne: 'Babel is a myth of the common people and the confusion of tongues exists only in the minds of the folk who like to imagine that there are several tongues because they have no thorough knowledge of their own. For anyone who knows how to read there is only one language in the world. For such a person, Babel never existed.'

"Another quality marks them apart—these dreams are as easily remembered as nightmares although they lack their elements of terror. They are vivid and persist in the mind for years even if one does not write them down. In fact, they usually waken the dreamer so they cannot be forgotten. They come at their own time and cannot be induced; probably they appear when they are most needed. They solve certain problems or show us our situation quite precisely, coming usually when life is frustrating and mean, when we are most miserable and most in need of guidance. They always involve the dreamer, either as the main character or the sole witness.

"They tend to tell it like it is and to have several layers of meaning. Our philosophical ideas will explain them if the philosopher is of great enough depth to follow them down but usually they are too deep for any man to understand. Spoken and written words are the first reliable type of information; dreams are the second. Their scenarios would do credit to Shakespeare and I strongly suspect they did inspire him. They come as a play all worked out to plot and action and characters. Their form has been lifted directly into our folk tales. You can see that a play or a story is more easily remembered than unconnected ideas, just as poetry is, and they may be prophetic. Rightly understood they may even predict the future and the relationships that will exist there."

He thought for a while, then decided to go on, as the intense attention on her face demanded it. "On the point of dream interpretation, Jung gives us some very cogent advice. Dreams have some special and significant function of their own. They exist as a reality and are not the product of or the result of work in the imagination. No one can make up a dream and especially a Type-3 dream, so only the material that is clearly and visibly part of a dream should be used in interpreting it. Treat the dream as a fact, make no previous assumptions except that it somehow makes sense, and always remember that the dream is a specific expression of the unconsciousness. The Talmud even says, 'The dream is its own interpretation.' These Type-3 dreams originate in a spirit that is not quite human, but is rather a breath of nature—a spirit of the beautiful and generous as well as of the cruel goddess. I do rather prefer my theory of Dream Angels to this cruel goddess of Jung, though. It seems much more tender and even lovelier."

"I agree. I love our Dream Angels."

"Above all, Jung says, it is plain foolishness to believe in ready-made systematic guides to dream interpretation, to buy a reference book and look up a particular symbol. No dream symbol can be separated from the individual who dreams it, and there is no definite or straightforward interpretation of any dream. But in the hands of an expert, meaningful and valuable interpretations may be derived. I think this is quite clear. Do you agree?"

"Yes," she said hesitantly.

"This is not specific to Type-3 dreams, but it appears most clearly here. They occur against the face of eternity so they are set in the immediate present or the immediate Now. They are not enmeshed in the time or the place of this time/dimensional continuum." He looked at her. "It is terribly confusing. Do not worry, Mrs. Darnely, we will go over all this again. I know it is a great draught to be taken all at once." He chuckled. "Like medicine, we will let you sip it a spoonful at a time."

"They prophesy the future? I thought the future was unpredictable." Her soft mouth formed the words reluctantly and her brow furrowed, for she feared to disagree with him.

"In truth the future is by and large unknowable and yet I believe you had some idea of my appearance before we met. Did you not see a man you would go anywhere with and one that showed you about on a ship? Was this not so?"

"I did meet a man who resembled you in many ways. He was, yes, I think so . . . well, it may have been you, I mean." She stammered.

"The first time we met in a dream my beard was brown, but at that time of my life it was, indeed, brown. The Angels of Dreams know more than we are privy to. They do have a plan for us, for mankind, for all life, and since it is an immortal plan we may depend on it for it is indeed a self-fulfilling prophecy. We can predict as much of the future as that plan allows to us. Dreams and visions are blazing signs, flashing benchmarks the Angels of Dreams use to guide us on that path. I think of those who receive these dreams as being under the control of fate or eternity, maybe even of the Angels themselves. Each of these dreams is a directing arrow. If we can follow these dream-leads we who labor at the philosophic forge may be more able to tread out our lives in the manner envisioned by our creator. Do you realize how much of our Bible concerns itself with dreams? Have you read Daniel and his marvelous visions? Of course you know of Joseph and the dream of Pharaoh that saved Egypt."

"Certainly, but I didn't realize other places in the Bible were full of dreams as well."

"Indeed they are," he said. "Listen!" His voice dropped to a resonant bass tone, "'When I say, my bed shall comfort me, my couch shall ease my complaint, then Thou searest me with dreams and terrifiest me through visions. How long wilt Thou not depart from me, nor let me alone till I swallow down my spittle? I have sinned; what shall I do unto Thee, O Thou preserver of men? Though He slay me yet will I trust in Him.'

"This section from Numbers 12:5-10 is about as perfect a reference to the theosophical use of dreams as I have found. 'And the LORD came down in the pillar of the cloud, and stood *in* the door of the tabernacle, and called Aaron and Miriam: and they both came forth. And he said, Hear now my words: If there be a prophet among you, *I* the LORD will make myself known unto him in a vision, *and* will speak unto him in a dream. My servant Moses *is* not so, who *is* faithful in all mine house. With him will I speak mouth to mouth, even apparently, and not in dark speeches; and the similitude of the LORD shall he behold: wherefore then were ye not afraid to speak against my servant Moses? And the anger of the LORD was kindled against them; and he departed. And the cloud departed from off the tabernacle; and, behold, Miriam *became* leprous, *white* as snow: and Aaron looked upon Miriam, and, behold, *she was* leprous.'"

"Do we have to follow this dream path?"

"Not at all. God invites; He does not command. Would you please take that Bible and read Isaiah 1:18?"

She read in a firm voice, "'Come now, and let us reason together, saith the LORD: though your sins be as scarlet, they shall be as white as snow; though they be red like crimson, they shall be as wool.'"

"Close the book!" he said in triumph. "Do you see that, Mrs. Darnely? How clearly does Isaiah state it. God lays out the path and suggests we follow it. But we have free will and God will not invade that. He shows us the way and makes firm our footsteps on the path. If we do not follow Him then we go another way. Many are called but few are chosen, as it says."

She suddenly sucked in her breath as she thought of the implications of these statements. "Then Type-3 dreams are something very special. I mean, very, very special."

"Yes, exceedingly special." He waited until she smiled her agreement. "But you asked what these dreams do?" He continued. "First they reveal our warp and our weft until we come to know every shining thread of the web that weaves our minds. Only a few are Type-3 dream receivers but these fertilize deep roots. Second, they march us to the quick time and the rhythms that bring the changes proper to their time. Third, they offer us the only possible escape from the slavery of illusion." He smiled grimly, "they allow us to become the slaves of infinity. Fourth, they show us in our actions, and that gift allows the true self-exploration. We know what we are like. We can do rash acts if we are rash, dangerous acts if we are brave; many, many other acts and motions in these dreams and not die from the consequences."

He smiled at her concentration as he gently scratched his beard with one long nail. "Yes, Mrs. Darnely, yes indeed. Very special. In fact, it is even more special than that. Let us suppose that you were a commander of troops. I know, it is difficult to conceive of a lovely lady being a troop commander but let us say you are. You would have two concerns, correct?"

"I suppose so."

"Certainly you would. You would want to be certain that your troops were loyal to you to death and that they understood and would carry out your plans exactly as you envisioned them. Would those not be your proper concerns?"

"They certainly sound right to me."

"To do this you would have to talk to them or have your officers talk to them?"

"Right."

"But think of the problems! While they are being addressed, are they not prone to fall asleep or to fall into reveries and miss your message? And how can you be sure that they have not shut off your words out of treasonous thoughts?"

"I can't, of course."

"Correct. So the best thing you could possibly do would be to contact and instruct them in their sleep. I am sure you are aware of these devices one puts under one's pillow to assist in learning?"

"Yes, I am. I tried one once but don't think it helped. I still did poorly on the exam."

"But if you could reach into your soldiers' sleep and give them your message would that not be a magnificent mode of information assurance? You have them at their lowest level of resistance to your ideas. You have their undivided attention. You can place the images so they cannot forget. So if the Angels of Dreams wanted to so instruct mankind would they not use this absolutely perfect method of communication?"

"Why yes, yes. I'd never thought of it that way before. They certainly would. Yes they would. Well! You certainly have put a great and new importance on dreams for me. Then I guess I shouldn't feel bad about talking about them."

"Quite the contrary, you should feel very honored

that they were given to you. They are of very deep meaning, and, you may be more of a soldier than you think."

"Can we back up here a moment?"

"Certainly."

"You said these Type-3 dreams single us out and give some indications of who we are. Can you enlarge on this?"

"Madam, I can enlarge on this until the morning light will wonder at our sanity that we would barter our precious sleep for such a sea of words." He raised his eyebrows.

"I would far rather listen to 'a sea of words' on this subject than sleep."

"Spoken like a true student. Very well. If we define life at its basic level we find it is a graded process of birth, increase in size, mixing of genetic material and death. That does not sound particularly thrilling to me."

She pursed her lips. "I hadn't quite thought of it in those terms but I admit when you look at it that way it is dull."

"You will also admit this is the basic scenario of all life on this earth?" She nodded. "Then what makes life so intense, vibrant, compelling? Why does it command our attention to such a degree that we will willingly give up our lives for life?"

She shrugged. "I guess I just always accepted it as compelling."

"No, there is a far stronger reason. There are two overwhelming illusions, the First Illusion and the Second Illusion; throwing dazzles of scintillating scrim that flash desire over our entire world. And these control everything. We have only the sad illusion of control that these great illusions condescend to us. Everything life does on this earth is driven by the First Illusion and in our species, it far outstrips the ridiculous. For the murmur of a dream, a promise in the loin, for these ephemera, Mrs. Darnely, we have overbuilt our beautiful planet with great stone cities, connected them with the most sophisticated machines,

gone to the moon and the planets, and we are only starting. One day we will finish the destruction of our planet
and then, it must be to the stars. Almost our entire human
race is so entranced. Who are these people? These are the
illusion driven. Until death do them part they yearn ever
more intensely for the thrills and absorptions and the
self-forgetfulness of this waking ecstasy that shimmers just
beyond their reach."

He was silent as she thought through these words.
"I guess I had no idea illusion was so pervasive," she said.
But I guess it was, is, I mean, my own life was driven by it
until I met a certain crocodile. Well then, if I have changed
my focus, others can too."

"Precisely. You went from illusion to illusion and
you are not alone. We choose our illusions. Some of us find
fascination in the Second Illusion, far more are entwined in
the First. Because within these two illusions are the activities that can gloss life and paint it meaningful and delirious.
Those who are destined to stand in the Second Illusion pursue philosophy, are ferreted out by dreams and fed on intox-
icating views. 'If there be a prophet among you, I the
LORD will make myself known unto him in a vision, and
will speak unto him in a dream.'"

"So, the dreams do this to us?"

"Yes. They find us, instruct us, whip us about from
face to face, and push us into a certain state—where death
itself is a relief of burdens laid down. I suspect you have not
read Plato's words that the eternal is a hunter of men. And
by 'men' here he clearly means men and women, or
mankind."

"No, I haven't read that place."

"I will try to find it for you so you can read it in
context at your next visit."

the serpent
of separation

June Darnely was in the family car and moving fast over a smooth road. Her father was driving, her mother was in front, and her brother and she were in back. As they crossed the bridge at Hood River where it runs into the Columbia, the car hit a bump and she suddenly flew out of the back seat. She knew they did not turn around, they did not even look in her direction, they just drove on across the bridge without her. She landed in the river shallows on her back; legs drawn up, arms tight to her sides, watching in blank dismay as the lights of her family car drove swiftly up the road without the slightest pause.

As it got smaller and smaller, the wrenching thoughts, "they didn't even miss me, they don't care," ached in her heart. She was too hurt to cry and too young to understand. What does the child know at eight?

She felt the cold water bunching up against her neck, running fast along her sides. The deep blackness of the night went on above her without moon or stars; just the slight luminescence of the sky where it warmed a bit on the earth. It seemed like an endless time of that black night and that empty sky and that cold water that bulged and chilled around her lightly clothed body. Tears broke suddenly as the anguish flushed from her eyes and the cold block of that intense separation ached in the vacuum of her chest. Then, she saw it!

She shuddered and recoiled backwards in intense loathing. There was a great, black, coiled serpent close to the left side of her head. She was forced to watch it coiling and uncoiling, the great muscles of its body slipping it through its convolutions as through the grease of cold terror. And the real motion of all this writhing of the ghastly thing was shoving it closer and closer to her. Its heavy, black, triangular, scale-shiny head was raised and weaving a Satan dance above the waters. Its eyes burned with a hideous yellow glaze and the cold red tongue lashed to and fro as it whipped in and out of its mouth. She was locked to those eyes, locked to their amber intensity that stared straight into her cringing pupils. The head moved more swiftly now, swinging its pendulum from side to side riding its hypnotic gaze, measuring her, suspended not six inches from her face, watching, lining up for its fatal strike. She tried to pull away, to get up, anything to escape from that balanced horror but her body would not move.

"It's a rattler! It's going to bite me! It's going to kill me!" She screamed in frenzy and tried desperately to move, but her body was riveted into that whirling water and the snake moved closer. It's mouth gaped open and the needle sharp fangs were aimed straight into her eyes. In the slow motion the frenzy of heightened awareness gives, it etched itself in microscopic intensity.

"It's striking! It's going to bite me!" she sobbed now in exhausted, screaming gasps, again and again.

It suddenly rammed the mass of its head straight toward her face. And just as suddenly the force of her lunge to move back from that hideous mouth brought her violently awake. The first hint of an eerie dawn came through the window.

"I was panting in terror in the cold bedroom, lying in a freezing pool of my own sweat, on my back with legs drawn up just as I'd been in the river. I was shivering until the whole bed shook and was holding my breath so hard my throat locked in spasm and I could barely force the air of my breath past my throat. My arms were suction glued to my sides; I literally had to peel them off my legs. This took some of the pressure off my chest and eased air into my lungs. The bedclothes were off, the blankets crunched up on my legs. Each narrow draught of air I dragged in scraped across my throat like the burn of quicklime. My neck muscles contracted, arcing the pain of their burning into my head and fiery throat. My heart pounded until the whole bed throbbed to its beat.

"Without realizing it, my fingers had been gripping hard into the mattress to hold onto the only substantial thing at hand lest somehow I lose hold on wakefulness and slip back into that river. One of my fingers was signaling the pain of a ripped-back nail. My eyelids were shocked widely open until my eyes burned in their dryness. I had even forgotten to blink in the extremes of that terror. Slowly, jammed with the fast pain of my slogging heart, the minutes ebbed away. Slowly, oh so slowly, my breathing quieted and my heart went not quite so fast, and the intense pain of its slamming beat grew a little less.

"I remembered with that sick shock the confrontation when I was four, running and skipping along a mountain path. The delight of the morning air, the rich pine smells, and the many little chipmunks and squirrels that appeared and disappeared had lured me quite far ahead of my mother. Just as I rounded a bend, I saw it—loathsome, iridescent green and slithering along the ground ahead of me. I stood horrified, nailed to that ground, I couldn't move my legs, my eyes locked onto that despicable thing. Then finally I got command of my legs and ran screaming back to my mother, face blanched and breath gone, clinging to her skirts and hoarsely shouting. Snake! Snake! Snake!

"My mother bent and swooped me up, holding my shaking body tight against her breast. She soothed and cooed until at last I could be put down. For the rest of my walk I had stayed very close and hung tightly to her hand. Even now I dread the mountain trails.

"Just the week before that dream my mother had read Genesis 3:1-6. 'Now the serpent was more subtil than any beast of the field which the LORD God had made. And he said unto the woman, Yea, hath God said, Ye shall not eat of every tree of the garden? And the woman said unto the serpent, We may eat of the fruit of the trees of the garden: But of the fruit of the tree which *is* in the midst of the garden, God hath said, Ye shall not eat of it, neither shall ye touch it, lest ye die. And the serpent said unto the woman, Ye shall not surely die: For God doth know that in the day ye eat thereof, then your eyes shall be opened, and ye shall be as gods, knowing good and evil. And when the woman saw that the tree *was* good for food, and that it *was* pleasant to the eyes, and a tree to be desired to make *one* wise, she took of the fruit thereof, and did eat, and gave also unto her husband with her; and he did eat.'

"My mother asked, 'do you know what happened next? What that evil serpent caused?' I said 'no.' My mother said, 'I'll tell you!' She was righteously indignant. She said, 'He threw them out of the Garden of Eden. That serpent is the reason we are still separated from the garden paradise.'

"I realized then, that it's a Serpent of Separation, that's what it is—a Serpent of Separation.

"I've pondered this beast for years. Serpent of Separation, it drummed over and over in my mind. Was this the cruel beast that attacked me? And what was it going to separate me from? I had no idea. . . ."

Dr. Zvee's voice broke into her concentration.

"Separations, separations, separations, in ones and twos and threes come to the dreamers of serpents, for the animal always bears that message. Have you been separated, Mrs. Darnely?"

"Oh, my, yes. Yes, indeed, I have. He has it all now. My brother has it all and I've been locked out of that family. What is this serpent and why does it separate and why is it so terrifying?"

"Because of the all of what it is. No arms, no legs, and yet it moves like sine-waved lightning across the water and the land. It is a light blazing of pure energy that vanishes into the grass. Its bite is one of the most lethal, some species inject a venom that kills in a few minutes. The cobra stands and flares its neck and prepares to strike as we might stand and bow our neck and prepare to strike and those who early saw the central nervous system—our brains and spinal cords that float in their own waters and do not really touch any part of the body they rule, connected only by the synapses that transmit their messages—realized the snake was a particularly apt symbol. Remember how it flared over the Buddha and blocked the rays of the sun with comforting shade? In fact the snake is always such a dense and important symbol because all of its symbolism is present all of the time."

"So it is not always bad?"

"Of course not. Nothing is either bad or good but as our minds perceive it."

She saw clearly now that even at age eight she and her family had separated. Her intense need to be alone, the tree at the far end of the yard with its comfortable lower branch where she sat to think out her life and how she lived, her intensities of difference, all branded her as separate. And age had drifted her further and further until there was no communication. But the one that ached until the pain cut clear to her back was that first separation. That plunged her into the vacuum of herself—it is not always lethal but it always changes the separated one intensely.

Dr. Zvee's voice gently interrupted her. "When you were reading that passage from Genesis did you wonder at the serpent's amazing erudition? How could he know what would happen if they ate of the Tree of the Knowledge of Good and Evil, that they would end up to be like God, knowing good and evil? Especially when God had told them they would die. How could he know all that?"

"I've wondered about that. I don't know how he knew."

"And yet the Bible tells us he knew."

"Yes, certainly."

"How like a wise soul was that animal. How sound was its counsel, if we could but understand its advice. How could it know what was only known to God? The serpent has slithered through our thought from a time that long preceded the Garden of Eden. And it is always confusing because all the levels of its meaning and symbology are always present at each moment of its appearance and it separates at each level.

"As a fertility symbol it held veneration in all the ancient moon capitals. It was the staff that became rigid in Moses' hand and flaccid when he released it. It brought about the first puberty when the child was so quickly elevated into the youth and rose in thought against the family: when the young victims were sliced from their nourishing familiar warmth under the red and the black of that burning.

"As the central nervous system it both divides and is divided. As the programmed and wise soul that knew all that God had not told Eve, it led to the ultimate dividing between Eden and Adam, Adam and Eve, Cain and Able, down all the 'begets' until now. And it approached you from the left or spiritual side." His eyebrows arched in wonder and he smiled. "And the automobile. Did you think of the automobile?"

She shrugged. "I suppose I had to get into that river some way and we would normally go by car." She looked into his waiting eyes that told her she had obviously missed the point. "Not so, huh? I guess I didn't really think about the car."

"We are prone to forget that in dreams we do not need to get into that river some way. The dream is perfectly capable of flying you there or just starting out with you in the river or handling it in a myriad ways we would never think of. Everything in such a dream is symbolic and necessary for the scenario. Think now of the car, is it not a perfect simulacrum of the core family? There are the parents and the children of those parents, that is the family. The father guides this one as yours was driving, the mother watches beside him and adds her counsel, nagging as some cynics say." He chuckled. "And the children follow. The dream gave you a rigid definition of your family. When you bounced out, you bounced out of that family. You bounced out because your father hit a bump. Did he make some major miscalculations in his business affairs at that time?"

She sucked in her breath sharply. "How did you know that?"

"I simply listened to the dream." He smiled.

"Yes, he bought a farm and that was a very bad thing to do. We really suffered on that farm, never had enough money, never enough to eat." She grew silent.

"At the point where you struck the river the dream went beyond your reality and played out against two of the densest dream symbols. And as is usual in these dreams, you were placed in the correct relationship to both of them. We have mentioned the snake, now let us concentrate on that river. You entered at a confluence where two great flows come together, the physical and the spiritual, male and female, Yin and Yang if you are conversant with Oriental philosophy, and become one in their path to the sea. And you landed on your back, Mrs. Darnely. Imagine that! On your back! This is because the river and your back are both the flow of the river.

"Have you thought of rivers or tried to define them?" She shook her head. "Could we say they are paths that divert water temporarily away from the sea so life may not be bound to the ocean? And you know of course that life may only live in water?" She nodded. "You agree that all land-life depends on those waters and most of the great civilizations have blossomed along river banks." She nodded again. "And rivers depend on the mysterious action of the air to absorb ocean water which is combed out by the mountains and brought to earth as rain. Mrs. Darnely, a miracle! All the rivers on earth flow into the oceans and yet the oceans are never filled. All the souls on earth flow into God and yet God is never filled. Until there appeared the human mind that communicates, that receives communication from other minds wherever they are, that sends the communication and answers it, until then the first infinity, the infinity without beginning and without end, God's infinity, was enough. The universe floated in its space without dimensions and God ruled His vastness.

"But humans pondered upon the rivers that ran continually until they ended in the seas, fed only by a blur of rain drops, by nebulous gatherings of foggy clouds showering down their airborne load which actually begins in the ocean. And the ocean—seas in their vastness humans saw as the waters of immensity that swim the stars and none of these waters have a beginning. Thus did the idea of a second infinity come to them. Human conceit divided an infinity from God's infinity and formed one that had no beginning but a definite end. We humans, minds modeled on infinite mind and the sparks from it, were and are the division points. Each of us terminates a second infinity. Even as we speak these words, its waters break against our backs. Eden of the garden fame means, as you would expect, a paradise. But it also means 'until now'.

vthing that has gone before terminates in that garden
ll of that is until now." He looked at her face to see
ncept slowly surface and firm up in her smile.

"Would you like to see this second infinity?"

"Yes!" she said eagerly. "Yes, I would."

"This small hand mirror will do. Hold it before your eyes and look over your left shoulder." He gave her a mirror five inches in diameter. "We are told we should look slowly that death may have time to move away. We should peer straight into the mirror with our mind's eye. For this view, the Sufis have a word, *Suliram*, which means exactly what you are doing: looking in a mirror to see all that is behind you. Do you see your mother and father standing behind you? Perhaps if you half close your eyes, change the mirror angle a bit, still no?"

In spite of flexing, extending, and contracting her arm: nothing. "I'm sorry. I just can't see anything but the wall." Her voice sighed in defeat. He let her struggle for a while longer. "Why do I have to use a mirror? Why can't I just turn my head?"

"Because when you turn your head you are not look-ing behind you, you are looking ahead of you."

"I don't believe I understand this."

"Let us first explain *Suliram*. Then we can go into the motion of the mind as it is related to the head. One day you may become an adept at mirror vision and you will see the chain of your generation. Behind your parents are your grandmothers and grandfathers and behind them your great grandmothers and great grandfathers and your mind will take you on and on and out and out, changing life forms to the more and more primitive until you finally realize that there is no beginning to that line. It extends to infinity and begins in infinity. The tail that leads to it and tells all that is your tale is behind you and sprouts from your coccyx, just like a good tail should. I am sure you have spent much time thinking of your back and your coccyx and your tale."

"Well, I suppose I have spent some time on it. I mean, it can hurt and I sure think of it then. But I've surely never thought of all the things you just said. What is a coccyx, anyway?"

"Why it is the beginning of the tail and the start of our tale and the end in our beginning of the beginning in our end. So much goes on in the back. It is the pine tree, the spine tree holding our heads up into the heavens. It begins as thirty-three soft cartilaginous forms that, by the age of twenty-six, have fully calcified and mightily strengthened and coalesced down to twenty-six hard bones. The male spine firms and stays firm unless he chooses to turn and become as a little child as Jesus mentioned but the female hovers all her life on the edge of decalcifying back to the child's estate. Your dream told you much about your back for it connected it to the river. Even before the serpent arrived, you were securely attached in that infinite flow." His smile was very reassuring.

"You mean, if the serpent had bitten me, I wouldn't have died?"

"No, you would not have died. You were a child and you had not calcified and sealed off your back, your place of crossing over, your Jordan of the infinite and holy. You were connected. You had roots that sank deep into that river that flowed from the infinite and holy. Do you remember how long you lay there before the snake came?"

"It seemed to be a very long time."

"Root time, Mrs. Darnely, root time. The snake's bite would have separated you from this life before you, from the life that hovers even between us now but the river would have sustained you through your back." She nodded as the earliest dawn of comprehension tinted her mind. He went on.

"That River of Union—where you will see all your ancestors from the very earliest and infinite time—is the same river Siddhartha hovered over so precariously, mesmerized by the infinity of life it carried to the sea."

"Because I was a child that river treated me differently?"

"Because you were a child that river was rooted to you. Now you are an adult and those roots have withered in the chalk of your bones."

"Being a child must be a very great thing."

"Being a child, having a child, just seeing a child, is a very great thing. The greatest estate is the estate of childhood and all children are in that state. They are the clay, perfect in form, perfect in function, that molds to the adult. They are loved everywhere. How marvelous of God to invent children! And what perfect packages of symmetrical accuracy they are!

"The river of waters is equally a river of life for it carries life and nourishes life, but it is even more: it is a symbol of the true river of life that ends on the back of Mrs. Darnely. When you become an expert at *Suliram* you will see this but for now just listen and follow its flow. Before viruses we do not know. So we will start with them, multiplying, changing a bit over time, adding to, until bacteria and algae and amoebae and all these simple and soft creatures were carrying the flow of life. Then the Cambrian and Ordovician and Silurian periods with an explosion of strange forms, 500 to 400 million years ago. And the DNA and RNA reproduced themselves and that unbroken line flowed on but it was different now. There were two sexes and increasingly complex modes of adding up this mass of nucleic acid, until, a million, two million years ago, some time, the right mix, and, voila! We began. Now when you use your mirror you see a river of DNA in form, an infinite extension of eggs and sperm regularly coalescing to rise into a human morph. Those protoplasmic bits flow through us until bias and position bring them together and more of us are born. If you know about mushrooms, you can see that the mycelia are equivalent to our river of union and we to the fruiting bodies. It sounds a bit racy when we say it that way." And he blushed lightly.

"All the ancestors behind you in your mirror are but standing in that river. Certainly, their bodies are air washed but the arch of reproduction is awash in the flow of potential life forms. We are born from the river into our parents' arms that hold us till our stance is strong, until we stand in our own power and we in our turn conceive in the river. We grow old, that river receives us, and our children are heirs to our power. These are the future and the exact future and all that the future may be. They are the beginning of yet another infinity, the third infinity, that has a beginning but no end and their progeny will go to that infinity."

A long silence settled between them while she sorted the images birthed from his voice. "What," she wondered, "makes it so compelling. It's sound is a cross between a hypermature bullfrog and sandpaper. And yet, when he speaks—"

She spun in her head, old sluice-ways unclogged and a scintillation of imagery dazzled the gates of her mind. She looked down her past with eyes of new comprehension. "Separation on separation on separation, just as it predicted. How wise that dream was!" she exclaimed.

"A great friend of mine dreamed a very similar dream about the River of Union. I believe it would be instructive to compare them. Would you like to hear it?"

"Oh, yes, very much."

"His began with the dreamer standing beside a great river. On his side, the bank was bare. On the other side was dense tropical forest. As he watched, the waters turned crystal clear revealing vast numbers of animals of all kinds down in the river hollow: mice and rats, baboons, gorillas, monkeys, insects and even a few humans. They were standing or moving about in no particular order; all forms of life flowed together. Then the water disappeared completely and the dry channel seemed to be a signal for all of them to start running. They ran pell-mell up the opposite bank and disappeared into the forest.

"The dreamer then turned from the river that had been water and now was life, that held all those living forms sweeping back to infinity. He went several yards from its bank. A perfectly circular pond about three feet in diameter was there that held such things as one might find in a tidal pool when the ocean leaves it: living corals and sponges and sea anemones. This small and stable pool was a magnifying light that brought into immobility and clear focus the hectic life that was running out of the river, where he could examine and analyze and hone his attention to the fine point. He was staring into its depths as the dream ended."

He smiled with the triumph of ideas logically passed as she said, "why that exactly describes what you said about the River of Union. And that's the same river I was lying in?"

"I am sure it was the very same river. The River of Union is a river of water, which is a river of life, which is a river of water, which is a river of union. The river is such a perfect example of what it is, that it is also a symbol of itself." They chuckled together.

"I may sound a bit paranoid, but do all dreamers have to start out with such dreams as this one? Isn't it possible to dream pleasant dreams?"

"In childhood it does seem the Type-3 dreams are very traumatic. Would you take that copy of *Memories, Dreams, Reflections* by C. G. Jung, and turn to page eleven please?"

She scanned it quickly. "It's a long section, goes on to the next page. You want all of it?"

"I'll describe it for you. Dr. Jung suffered intensely to bring us this stunning dream.

"When he was only between three and four years

old he dreamed he was in a big meadow where the vicarage stood quite alone near Laufen castle. He discovered a dark, rectangular, stone-lined hole in the ground and a stone stairway leading down. At the bottom was a doorway with a round arch, closed off by a green curtain. He pushed it aside and saw a rectangular chamber about thirty feet long. In the center, a red carpet ran from the entrance to a low platform. On this platform stood a golden throne. Something was standing on it, which he thought at first was a tree trunk twelve to fifteen feet high and about one and a half to two feet thick. It was made of skin and naked flesh, and on top there was something like a rounded head. On the very top of the head was a single eye.

"It was fairly light in the room, as above the head was a brightness. It did not move, yet he had the feeling that it might creep toward him. He was terrorized. At that moment, he heard his mother's voice. 'Yes, just look at him. That is the man-eater!' He awoke sweating and scared to death. For many nights he was afraid to sleep, because he feared he might have another such dream." Dr. Zvee's voice ended.

He finally broke the silence. "Did his pain match yours, Mrs. Darnely?"

"Yes," she whispered. "In fact, it was worse. I never got to where I couldn't sleep. Poor man. Poor child. That's what I mean. Why did he have to have dreams like that?"

"I believe the real answer lies beyond us but it may be as simple as saying; without that dream there would be no Carl Jung. Would that be an excessive stretching of the truth?"

"No, of course not. I suppose that's what they do, these great ones. They suffer more than the rest of us and they throw up the challenge for us to suffer and shut up about it."

Dr. Zvee smiled broadly. "There is a very profound truth in what you say; the great ones are concerned to set an example for the weaker brethren. If Jung can go through that we can certainly bear the pain of our own lives." He mused over the image for awhile. "You know what the gold means, the force that floats and passes into the intellect. And you know the red refers to the blood and the passions on which it rests. Jung was surprised to find what the large and fleshy pillar was that rose from the throne. And remember, he found all of this underground."

"The light and the eye are significant?"

"Extremely. The light is the life of man and the eye sees upwards and illuminates its own path from the darkness of its surrounding hole. It is this that brings light into the caves of dead matter; this that guides man both into and out of this world. And it is that light and that eye that look into themselves that fill their whole being full of light. 'If thine eye be single then shall thy whole body be full of light.'"

corollary dream
by Silene Frank, age forty-three

She was in comfortable clothes walking in a large treeless meadow in the new morning. It was early summer and the sun was up and warming everything. A hill rose in the east. The air was humid and hot and fertile, as even the tall grass and weeds smelled of their insistent greenness. When she was about to leave, she came upon a hut. It was four feet high and a perfect hemisphere and its door faced away from the rising sun. The structure was primitive, made of a skeleton of thatch that showed in places through the roof but mostly was covered over with clay, which seemed to have been troweled on with a rough hand. The door to this hut was a small arch covered with a very dark brown coarsely woven cloth that pulled to one side.

When she saw this dome, she became anxious, for she knew she must go inside and had no idea what was there. Finally she knelt down, shrugged her shoulders and crawled in. Coiled in a loose coil in the middle of the round floor was a large, beautiful, black and pulsating fat snake that literally throbbed in the surges of its vitality. Its belly was a shimmering bluish white, its head swelled slightly out from its body, its tongue licked in and out and a small gold crown clung regally above its blue eyes. She was delighted and in awe for she knew it would not harm her, in fact it was a part of her very self. She looked for a long time literally mesmerized but she knew she had to leave.

Outside the grass was trodden in a primitive path that she followed to the north. There was another identical hut. She knew this was just for her also and she entered it quite willingly, as her first experience had been so positive. Again there was a black snake in the center but this one was not like the first. It was smaller, had no crown, pulsed not at all, and neither did it throb. There was certainly no incentive to spend any extra time in this hut. All was dull here and predictably and decidedly ho-hum.

She backed out, followed the path north and found the third hut. Nervous with anticipation of what may be there for her, she pulled the rough cloth aside and looked in. A snake was lying around its inside perimeter, its head almost against the north edge of the door as though it had been trying to escape or get more air. It was a dull gray-brown, its belly was light gray and it seemed to be near death like something about to decompose. She was grieved, but more than that she felt responsible for the condition of this poor animal. She thought she'd gotten here too late. She knew she was causing this snake to die, or at least allowing it to, but how could she revive it? And these sad thoughts brought her fully awake.

"So what does all this mean, Dr. Zvee?" Mrs. Frank asked.

"How many months later did you begin to plan your return to school?" Dr. Zvee countered.

"Oh, one, maybe two months," she answered.

"But before that you had no plans to return to school?"

"No, I really didn't have."

"Aha!" He chuckled. "So you needed me not at all. You took precisely the proper corrective action."

"I did?" she asked dubiously.

"Indeed you did. Do you not see it? No? Well then, let us examine this lovely and most instructive dream so you can follow its symbols. The meadow scene was full of fruitfulness and the burgeoning of life; that would suggest you were projecting it from an appropriate bodily place. There were paths to guide you though they were quite primitive and marked only by the trodden grass. Your dream did not ask more of you than a comfortable following of these. You faced east, so your huts faced west and lined up from north to south. You began at the most southern one precisely where Castaneda would have started you. The snake in that hut throbbed with life and wore a golden crown. No, Mrs. Frank, you certainly do not need to worry about your soul and your spirit. They are burgeoning and almost overwhelming in their vitality."

"That snake was my soul?"

"Almost in its entirety. Philo Judaeus describes the snake as that soul energy that attaches the soul to its sensations. And since sensations are fun and enjoyable, that makes them evil and gives the reptiles quite a bad press. You cannot imagine how dead this life would be if the serpent did *not* attach our senses, can you?" He smiled at her. "No, you could not imagine that. But you do have a most luxurious soul serpent and we may conclude your spiritual life is alive and throbbingly well. Is it not remarkable how the dream pictures, with such remarkable clarity, images of those things that really have no image, that exist only as energy fields, things such as our souls?"

"Yes," she mused, "quite amazing. I would never have thought of my soul as looking like that. Is that the way the biblical snake looked?"

"I would surmise he resembled your snake very closely. It will please you to know that your reptile was quite as wise as his ancient predecessor. And your snake was crowned in gold while it says nothing about such nobility in Genesis. But when you entered the next hut you were quite anxious to leave and actually very bored. That was a reptile of logic and day-to-day rationality; the arbitrator of the dull and pedantic thoughts men tend to inflict on their wives. An apathetic snake; a dull snake. Does it surprise you to learn that this snake is the understanding of the mind?"

"I guess it really doesn't. I know very well how absolutely ho-hum rationality can be when carried to the macho extremes you men affect." She paused for a few breaths and said, "I surmise the last one, that poor sick one that yanked so hard on my heart, *that* one is my brain?"

"Yes, it is your nervous system and you already know what it needs and how to strengthen it."

"By registering in school."

"Exactly! And by taking courses that demand of your intellect. Courses that require Herculean feats of capacity arrangement of your memory and much analytical thought. These gird up our brains against the onset of the dreaded Alzheimer's disease. These are the weight lifting and the long distance running designed to keep the central nervous system strong and throbbing against its meninges."

"My soul and my soul-snake then, are really where

I live. That's why that snake is so fat and vibrant?"

"Yes. And the mind and its understanding snake are dull and predictable. They are no fun, Mrs. Frank, no fun at all. You are anxious to get out of there and find the next hut. And when you do you find that reptile is dying. Can you now see that it is dying because of the neglect you have shown to the second hut and its animal. To save your brain you must learn to expand the hard intellectual logics and the syllogistic power of the second hut."

"In other words, I *have* to go to school!"

"Well reasoned. Very well reasoned." A comfortable silence followed.

Finally, she said. "I was facing east. I entered the huts through a western door. Can I picture myself lying on my left side and entering the huts through the back of my head?"

"Indeed! I believe that is the exact position that you are cast in by this dream."

37

chapter two

youthful dreamers

fter watching a particularly long and bone-chilling game, sitting on hard bleachers with no back sup- port, amazed at the immense effort that drove the helmeted and oddly bulging young men strutting and jumping and displaying on the muddy grass and wonder- ing why she could not sympathize with all that, she stood for a long while in her backyard as the intensity and reality of being all alone seeped into her marrow. At fourteen the heightened perceptions of puberty were ripping at her mind and ripening the serpent's promise.

June walked out into the fields toward her Blue Mountains that made the western sky jagged. She strained up her eyes in wonder and envy. Still was that night, for the nights of the northland *are* still. And they are whipped with cold and with great lights that play and jerk across the freezing sky while the stars stand out and watch with spotlight eyes. The stars that were so peaceful on this still night and so obviously without care and she had so little of the one and so many of the other. There was no cloud to cushion her longing from their hard star infinity, no moon to secure her sanity and they riveted into her head in their millions like diamond blinking steel nails blazing so close now above her. So close, so close, a position that brimmed with the thrill like that of a union. Fatigue finally came and forced her inside. It dimmed her eyes but she still lay long and wakeful on the hard mattress. Then she was whipped into sleep's first delirium as vertigo whirled her suddenly weightless body and she was off, swinging high up into that night sky.

The very stars were reaching and her heart in harmony was swelling up to match their call. Up, up, up, higher and higher. How far beyond the earth could her body soar? Her eyes coming closer, closer to the velvet black that held those enticing myriads of light points. Beyond the skimming northern lights and untroubled by their rays, all space was an intensity of black night for even the moon was wrapped away into the thick of that infinite deep. And then . . . she thought she saw those stars begin to move.

Slowly in a grand and stately cosmic dance they moved. At first, so slowly she was not sure. It could have been an aberration of her eyes but then they moved a little more rapidly. They seemed to be going at random and tracing no discernible pattern. They were playing with her, dancing surely to further the joy that they gave, dancing more wildly and arcing across the face of the firmament. And as they steadily gained the loci where it seemed they must settle, her eyes began to make out some form. For it became steadily more obvious that they were moving together to form a tremendous head, a head vast in expanse but one that was almost human. Yes, in the shape of a man's head—a man that bent all across the bowl of the heavens and stretched from horizon to horizon. Was this cosmic wonder staged just for her delectation? For her who was helpless, weak and tiny: a pale and insignificant eye in the straws of immensity. Was God's entire universe forming just for her?

And when the stars stood still and that great face of a very deep and brick red that colored into black only to shimmer again up to that dark red, that vast face was fully formed and its vast eyes opened gradually in the luxury of infinite time. She saw it full-face and it was grotesque and homely. As though it stretched itself out of a long, deep sleep the eyes opened and the face began to swell with the black-red power of its life. Alive and searchingly alive, it scanned with sweeping arcs of those baleful star-blazing eyes, searching, searching. Trembling seized June and her heart squeezed away her breath. Could it be she that it sought? And the terror built like an ominous grip that shaped up its talon for ripping.

Its head moved to follow those eyes in their seeking. Horribly it was moving, very slowly but as inexorably as the very gates of hell, straight toward her! Slowly, ever slowly, and with infinite power, it swept itself out of its chaos and clamped the vast intensity of its eyes on hers. It moved down on her, growing larger and larger and spreading its deep red until it claimed more than the sky and only its face was visible across the total expanse of heaven. But she was bolted in place in that terrible immobility that should happen only in dreams: she was merely a bust, her arms and her legs were gone and there was nothing to lever her strength to help her away from that face.

She could not look away and she watched, whipped ever higher toward that great mouth. Her legs tried to run, her arms tried to pump, but there were no arms or legs. There was nothing to grip with her feet had she had them, and not even futile air to flail about with her hands, for her earth was far below. Suspended, she dared not look down to see how high she hung. Nor could she have, for her eyes themselves were locked by the head power that suspended her. And her eyes watched the star eyes grin and crinkle in their lust and saw the mouth curve into a predatory smile. They leered down on her with the cannibal thirst and she knew in the certainty of her heart—*she* was that prey. *It was going to eat her!*

Its vast mouth opened and gaped to a star-studded, pulsating hole. The hunger eyes lusted with appetite. She would be ground in that terrible maw, swallowed into the emptiness of forever. She struggled in fierce mind spasms trying to move, to back away. But that weakness and lethargy that paralyze the body when the soul runs wild ruled her will and she could but flail in her mind and flounder in her brain. Her head was paralyzed and her eyes locked onto its mouth. Closer and closer it came, that gaping-toothed cave, opening slowly, slowly, closer and closer and she knew then it was all over. A morsel for hell was her doom and her portion.

Closer into the gaping maw of demoniacal terror, its mouth smiled intense anticipation, opened slowly even wider, its breath caught her on its current and she swept toward it. All of her vision was bound by its mouth, its vast teeth shining of hard star steel, and its tongue, thick and star puffed, hungrily licking up to her body. Beyond that tongue yawned the black infinity of her damnation.

She woke violently to a heaving heart and fear damped breath. She could control neither breath nor movement. It seemed to take hours before her heart realized its safety and her breathing came again under control. Sitting on the edge of the bed and staring into the still, black and moonless night, she surveyed that room. She forced her mind to a detailed analysis of every piece of furniture, spot, blemish, bruise—everything she knew so well in this one place that was hers.

She worked to rebuild with her intellect what the dream had stripped away from her thought, the feeling of the reality and the comfort of the familiar. But the dream tipped the far greater weight and she was cast even deeper into that soft gelatin of unreality that was born with the Serpent of Separation. Both dreams were locked in memory. Both were year-proofed by the steel strapping of fear.

"You sustained the onslaught of that dream at age fourteen? It is truly amazing what some persons can bear and even recover from, especially the females of our species." He sighed and shook his head in admiration.

"You agree that women can take much more than men?"

"Absolutely. Were that not so, the agonies of childbirth would have ended the human line before it began. Women are far more enduring of pain and all types of discomfort than men."

A prolonged silence intensified the anxiety in June's heart. She blurted out. "But what does it mean? What's it all about? Why did I have to go through that?"

"It bothered you a great deal?"

"For months I was afraid to go to bed. I fought sleep like a demon as I was so terrified that face would return."

"Then it had a very profound effect on your life."

"Extremely profound." She sat forward on her chair.

"Could you be more explicit?"

She sighed and slid into a more comfortable position. "Certainly. I had always had a very good sense of direction. I knew where I was. When my friends and I would go exploring in the hills, I was the one who brought us back when the others were lost. You could take me to strange country and new places and I would form some kind of mental map and inevitably get back home. I was that way with time, too. I always knew almost exactly what time it was, hardly ever needed a watch. That all got messed up after that dream. I would be sitting in my own front room and have a sudden bout of panic that I couldn't be sure where I was or what day it was. I didn't dare go exploring any more. I tried it a couple of times but I felt really unsure and I did get lost, I mean, really lost. That time my folks looked for me until late in the evening and that really upset them. And my sense of time was gone for sure. I finally had to get a cheap watch."

"So it broke the cage of your dimensions and left you shattered. How long did that disorientation last?"

"Oh, three, four months. By the time school was over I was all right. But I never again felt really good about going into strange country." Her brow furrowed. "You said it broke the cage of my dimensions? What did you mean by that?"

"Of course you know about the three spatial dimensions at right angles to each other."

"Up and down, to and fro, side to side, yes."

"Did you know that Einstein had added another?"

"I'd heard something about a mysterious fourth dimension. Didn't it have something to do with time?"

"Yes, exactly. There are four dimensions that are necessary to localize a point and the fourth is time. What is not so well known is the effect of these four dimensions on our minds. These to some extent imprison us, or it might be better to say they protect us, so we cannot go out to the night sky and see vast and terrifying black/red heads that fill the heavens." He smiled at her. "And threaten to eat us." Her answering smile was less than heartfelt. "As long as we are in good health and in the four dimensions, we have an accurate sense of space and time. When we are torn out of our dimensions, we lose that sense."

"Is this a common situation?"

"Quite common. Alcohol, drugs, isolation, changing time zones, jet lag as it is called, all these and more will unseat us from our four dimensions. Not only do we lose our sense of time and space but we also are severely hindered in our ability to remember and to think syllogistically. But unless we are able to unseat from the dimensions we are not able to see such visions as your Superman of Stars."

"Which is better? Getting scared out of your mind or not seeing such things? You know, if I had any choice in this, I would just as soon have some quiet nights of sound sleep. I honestly don't see the value in such terror."

His jaw set and he nodded slowly. "We know certain things. We know that nature is conservative and does nothing without reason and use. We also know that the major impediment between man and God is that man's mind is rigidly attached to the four dimensions. Of course, this must be for the orientation of that mind. But it is equally important to approach God from the standpoint of His reality. And that reality demands that we understand, or if we do not understand at least that we know. He is totally beyond the material and the dimensional world. Let us look at the remarkable experience of yours. Whether for better or worse we may not say, but your Superman of Stars is very close to an actual vision of the infinite. It may in fact be a view of an image that swims in infinity.

"I am sure you remember the great place in the Bible where it says that man was created in God's image, in the image of God created He him, male and female created he them. Two of those three creations took place in that image, the creations of the immaterial. We could call them the mind and soul. Think of this! In the very image of God. Is it given to man to see that image? If so, it must be extremely rare and may be possible only in the protected dream state.

"Carlos Castaneda describes seeing what might correspond to it. He was almost violently attracted and indulged himself far beyond the comfort level of his mentor, don Juan. The Cabalists talk of it but I do not know how many have seen it. They call it Macroprosopus, the great face or the divine face in heaven, compared to microprosopus, the small face, man's face on earth. The two faces are exactly correspondent. Hermes Trismegistus asserts that it is true, no lie, and to be depended upon: everything above corresponds with everything below. Everything that emanates from the great face impinges on the small one, nourishing, instructing, and yes even dreaming, that the small one may follow the path to the great one.

"But let us think in a more material and scientific manner for a moment. Einstein told us that time is inversely proportionate to speed. At the speed of light time slows to nothing. Now we know that the universe is filled with light, which we call the isotropic black body background radiation at 2.726 degrees Kelvin. So this and all other light is timeless. Therefore, anything that reaches such speed has already slipped beyond time. If greater speed were possible, the next step would be infinity. And we say that greater speed is possible because Marcel Duchamp tells us that God may go from one end of His universe to the other in an instant without any expenditure of time. He can do this because He is infinite, and infinite space exists in Him and His movements are at infinite speed. If all this is true would not that black body radiation be the bridge over to infinity? And it could even be the plane where an image of infinity is formed?"

"What you're telling me is that I saw directly an image from infinity. Can we say, projected?"

"We will have to use words like projected, for we are but mortals after all, on the plane of that black body radiation." He looked at her with amusement glinting behind his eyes. "Yes, I am saying that what you saw may have been a projection of infinity, perhaps an angel."

"Or a demon! That face most certainly did not look angelic. That was the homeliest, I mean the ugliest face I've ever seen."

"Infinity viewed through mortal eyes rarely appears beautiful."

"Besides, the face was made of stars and they are not eternal."

"The face was made of a pattern of stars, correct?"

"Yes."

"And it was colored a deep black/red. Could we call that color a brick red?"

"Yes, we could."

"The pattern and the color were the elements that gave it form, rather than the stars themselves?"

"Yes. I would say the stars merely outlined the image."

"Then, let us reason together for a moment. Our philosophers tell us that the world we see is built on a divine plan that we cannot see. If you wish to read about this, consult the first chapter of Philo Judaeus. The divine plan exists in eternity. From our vantage point we cannot see it. But suppose we were in the light of that black body radiation. Could we see it from there?"

She pushed her lips tightly together in the intensity of her thought. "I suppose, yes, I suppose we could. Certainly we would see things much differently than we do here traveling at this very slow speed."

"Exactly. I think everyone would agree that we would see things much differently. Now, Mrs. Darnely, what was in motion in your dream? You or the stars?"

"Well, both. Yes, I was moving up to them, but they were moving too."

"Have you ever seen a demonstration of the change in view as one accelerates to light speed?"

"No." Her voice was tense as her ears strained for his words.

"It is very interesting. The faster you go the more quickly you intercept the light waves and that puts all you see into motion."

"So perhaps the stars weren't moving? I was moving?"

"'If the soul could fling the clay aside and naked on the heavens ride, . . . ' as Omar Khayyam wrote. What is your soul velocity? Is there a celestial speed limit? Are your dreams launching pads that accelerate you—perhaps even beyond light speed? Did you peek over the sea of that light and look into an infinite world? Was it the infinite plan outlined as the Superman of Stars?" His voice was soft and tense and filled with the wonder of the images he provoked.

Barely able to speak from the weight of her sudden insight, she whispered, "and all that could have been what I dreamed? Great merciful heavens."

The smile slowly returned to his face as he moved to bring the cooling humor on her over-driven thoughts. "Now just to prove you really understand, tell me: which side is God's heart on?"

"Well." She relaxed and sat back in her big chair. "If we're made in His image we must be mirror images of Him. So I would guess it would be on His right. But, does He have a heart?"

"Are you saying that our God of love has no heart?" he cried in an accusing voice, carefully modulated by a softening smile.

"Oh, no, Dr. Zvee, I'm not saying that. I'm just saying that, well, I mean, does God have a heart? I mean, He's not like us . . ."

"Now how can you say that when not twenty minutes ago we preened ourselves on being created in His image?" And his smile swelled to a full, chuckling laugh. "Reason would say of course that you are quite right, but actually God's heart would have to be on the left as ours is on the left and that is because we are the descendants of His mirrored likeness. The one we meet in our mirror is the one we have descended from." He leaned forward in his straight chair as she looked at her watch.

"Good heavens, we've talked all afternoon. Where does the time go?"

"As the Romans used to say, 'Tempus fidgets when you are having fun.' His voice rose in excitement. "But tell me, Mrs. Darnely, have we not gone a long way on this dream? Perhaps a good and sound night's sleep would be more pleasant and far less strain to the nervous system, but it never would have stimulated such a conversation. Would you believe that we have been eating with the gods this afternoon?"

"Yes, Dr. Zvee, I would, uh, believe it. Indeed, we have been eating with the gods." Her voice was flat and unconvincing as her mind rummaged among the dream images. "I'm ungrateful. I'm unappreciative. In your eyes I've been given a great gift. But it almost drove me bonkers! Why did it have to be so terrifying?"

His voice was very gentle and his words came slowly. "It is hard to understand that the Angels of Dreams were doing you a kindness. They were letting you glimpse the dark side of eternity that you not over-love the brilliance of its bright side. The universe is adorned in the light of celestial fire and that can be a fulmination of madness. Only when we see it in the roundness of its parts do we temper our love. Think at what speed you whirled to the plane of your stars!" She nodded slowly.

"Robert E. Lee said at least once, 'It is good that war is so terrible or we should become too fond of her.' How, I used to wonder, could one become fond of war. War is killing and that is a terrible thing. But then I came more to understand his words. War is an absolute as love is an absolute. To enter either field you must put it to the test to win or lose it all. You live or you die. There is no mealy half-way measure here. It is all or nothing. It is the challenge of command of position demanded by chess, played on the sixty-four squares of a battlefield where the pawns drop to the earth and bleed into the ground of death. It is the strength, excitement, command, precision, power of massed troops, the heroism and cowardice, slaughter and death. All your life you live and ask for proof that you live. At the moment of war you die with the blood of the proof in your hand. War and infinity and love are the absolutes. They are the passions and inflammations of the young and we quickly become overly fond of them all."

After a carefully calculated silence, he asked very gently. "Mrs. Darnely, was the dream worth its cost?"

She stared straight ahead and weighed the question for some time before she decided not to answer.

corollary dreams: Sophia, age fifteen

Three or four times this dream recurred when she was twelve and thirteen. Each time she broke suddenly into the same landscape and found herself running at exhaustion speed on a brown gravel path about four feet wide. There was light enough to see the path and the world that hung tightly about her, which was glowering in the heat of shifting blacks and reds. She knew the Devil was chasing her. She knew he was close behind for almost at her ears the sound of his snorting and grunting warned of the immense efforts he was making to bridge the distance to her spine. Closer and closer crunched the rapid rhythm of his little feet. Suddenly she came to a wooden bridge and her shoes thundered across it. For a dizzy instant, she looked over the bridge railing down into a vast black infinity of endless deeps and chaotic voids. Then she left the sounding wood for the soft grass footing of the fertile land. At that moment, the very moment she left the bridge, the dream ended and she awoke with a pounding heart and racing mind.

At fourteen she dreamed she lay in the cupped hands of God. She knew she was in His hands because they were like no others: so vast and yet so tender and warm and cushioning. The entire universe seen through those hands was an evolving certainty of fulfilling promise. No words, no sound but she was sure it was He and if she walked in His ways she would be safe and protected all her days and would come to Him at the moment of separation from her body.

She lay on her right side bent at her hips and knees as comfortably as she had floated in her mother's womb. A large Bible, opened precisely in the middle, was lying on her left hip. It began to unfold and unfold and unravel and started to wrap around and around her slowly metamorphosing into a rather itchy brown wool blanket that did not quite cover her completely. The palms of the great hands moved slowly apart and she started a long, long fall. Now she was cold. She pulled her legs hard against her belly and tried to hold the blanket more snugly about her. For a long time she fell and then she hit something soft that did not hurt at all and she woke up to find a wonderful peace and harmony walking now where the dream had walked.

How good she felt! How warm and comfortable was her bed. How very very good the dream had been, and was, and would be—for all the comfort, warmth and sheer delight of it was with her at every instant of recall. When she told it to her one best and most carefully selected friend all the pleasures doubled. Was this the reason the Devil never chased her again?

In that same year she found herself in a desolate place and had a water glass in her right hand. A man was trying to get it from her but she flew up and over a great cathedral. Then she glided back to earth and gave up a round plate she was carrying and found that now she could not fly well. She walked a short distance over a bridge that crossed the empty void and then she could fly again with power. She flew now like a strong flying bird of great freedom over the tops of forests of trees. As she awoke the bird-feeling faded and she longed for it.

In October of the year she turned fifteen, she was again running hard on feet of lead and legs like iron pipes that bent only with incredible effort. She was pursued in terror by a large and very muscular man until fatigue forced her to stop and face him. As he lumbered toward her she could see he was stripped of all skin. His muscles were thick lumps that pulled at his joints and his face was a masked bone tensed into anger. It looked like a grisly picture out of an ancient anatomy text. He was slick and gooey all over with a thick white slime. She fought with him and found she was stronger than he. She threw him to the ground and awakened with triumph in her heart.

Again in October, she was in a cave with stalactites and stalagmites. All was dark and black and red and full of the tumult of demons. It was a devil world but in the midst of the cave, she found a black spinning chamber and when she entered it she was turned to a cartoon world full of green grass and carrots and many white rabbits.

"What is your impression of the time span of these dreams? They covered about two years?" Dr. Zvee asked.

Sophia's small round face moved into a quick, animated smile. "Yes, if I have my dates right, about two years. It was a very disturbing time. I mean I was all tense inside and there were things happening in my body I simply did not understand. But I guess it's something we all have to go through."

"It is indeed. Do you feel differently now than you did before?"

"Yes," she continued, encouraged by his eyes. "I'm more aware, more awake, maybe."

"Can you think of any other descriptive terms?"

"I know more now, lots more. I can concentrate better."

He let the silence build. "Have you thought that you might be more conscious of yourself? Self-conscious, as we say?"

Her mouth closed firmly and her eyes looked back into the feelings of her mind. "Yes," her voice raised. "Yes, that's it. I'm aware of myself. I can see myself and before that I really wasn't aware of me. I'm very much aware of me now. That's what you call self-conscious?"

"It certainly sounds like it. And that gives you the power to remember what you wish. Correct?"

"Yes," she said long and drawn out. "Yes. I can. And I have some control over my life now that I didn't have then." A large smile moved clear across her face.

He chuckled. "That time is a trying time but the rewards are great. Did you know it has been conjectured in scholarly circles that all mankind was in the pre-conscious state prior to about 500 BC? Even the *Iliad* was written by unself-conscious men. Then mankind woke up and children have matured in that pattern and into consciousness of themselves since that crucial time. But what is of greatest interest is that your waking-up-time seems bracketed by your dreams." He paused for a few moments. "And it seems to have been strongly influenced by them. Does it look this way to you as well?"

"Yes, I believe those dreams were a very strong influence."

"They began with the Devil chasing you out of the black/red land and the turning machine in the cave turned you out of a black/red place. One could conjecture that it may have been the same place. Can you see, on one level, that place might be the kingdom of childhood?"

"And he was chasing me out of it?"

"That seems to be a very real possibility. He was chasing you out of childhood."

"So his chasing me was a good thing?"

"Good in that context. You, Sophia, most certainly did not want to stay there forever. Although," he partly closed one eye like sharing a secret. "There seem to be those who *would* stay there if the choice were theirs."

"But why the darkness?"

"Because you yourself could not focus your child-mind, perhaps. And when you think back on those days of your dreams, do they not appear a bit foggy? Certainly mine do but that might be so because of my exceedingly advanced age."

"Dr. Zvee, you're not that old!"

"For that statement, my young friend, my heart is eternally grateful."

She frowned and he let her thoughts deepen. "What did I actually meet there in those years?"

"You actually met your womanhood. You met the person in the body, in the basement of your soul. In that turgid soup of emotions, passions, sensations, words and desires, you met yourself and you found out quite precisely who you are. You gained a name and it was Sophia, for in that which is wisdom you are wise."

Her face reddened and pinked and her smile trembled on the borders of her mouth. "But there's so much I have to know! Tell me! Tell me! Go through each dream and tell me!" And her eyes begged to learn.

"The Devil, Satan, the Accuser, the Eternal One. Did you know there are times he meets with the Lord? No? Read the first chapter of Job and you will be even wiser. And he goes up and down upon the earth and to and fro within it. Most important, the Lord points out the perfect man, Job, and allows Satan to tempt him. You heard him panting and snorting and it is widely rumored that he has a large nose, indeed, and you describe his 'little' feet running after you. You know, of course, that he has been described as having the feet of Pan. Then you reach the bridge of wood. Do you know about wood?"

"It comes from trees and we build things out of it."

"Quite correct. Also the tree stands perpendicular to the earth as does the spine of mankind. It is the third dimension. Small wonder the same Hebrew word means tree and spine."

"And that bridge went over a deep, deep chasm. There was no bottom or end to it and then I was on grass. That felt neat."

"And once beyond the bridge the dream ended, for Satan could not follow you over its boards. The bridge is to him a graven barrier that he is not allowed to cross. That black/red world is his and he is confined therein. Clear so far?"

"Yes."

"Sophia, always beware of elderly men who speak in hyperbole. But . . ." he stared with his lips pressed together and slowly scratched his beard, " . . . but, I am tempted to say that the next dream was the most beautiful I have ever heard. It was a benediction, a blessing and a comforting prayer. Imagine! You may know that the Bible is also called the Word of God. The Bible opened and opened until it surrounded you and became a brown wool blanket. Wool comes from sheep, possibly not from lambs when they are small, but certainly from lambs when they mature. Can you connect this with the Lamb of God that is so beautifully used throughout the New Testament?" She nodded, sitting tensely erect on the edge of her chair. "In the hands of God you were wrapped in the Word of God which became wool from the Lamb of God and thus you were allowed to float gently to earth, buffered from the cold of separation from Him. And you were given the unspoken assurances that you would return to Him if you followed His path. My, my." Again he meditated. "Would it not be enlightening to hear the dreams of the saints? How many were so benefited?"

"Can't we read them?"

"I do not know where they are written down." He smiled at her. "We have talked for some time. Are you weary? Would you like a refreshment?"

"I want to hear more about my dreams. Please tell me more."

"Very well if you promise to tell me when you are fatigued. Have you thought of a name for your blanket?"

"No, do you have one?"

"Quite a good one, I believe. Is not a blanket both an envelope and a wrapper?"

She shrugged. "It certainly seems so."

"Then let us name it 'Lot' for that is exactly what the name means."

She giggled. "That's neat. I'll call my brown woolen blanket Lot." She looked down at herself. "Hi, Lot!" And grinned some more. "But wasn't Lot a person in the Bible?"

"Certainly. He was the nephew of Abram. Terah had three sons, Abram, Nahor and Haran. Haran was Lot's father but he died in Ur of the Chaldees and Terah took his son Abram and Abram's wife Sarai and his grandson Lot to Haran. There Terah died. Abram faithfully took care of Lot and when famine forced him to journey to Gerar and Egypt he went along. Only when Abram returned safely from Egypt did he part from his nephew who chose Sodom. The further tribulations of this remarkable man, his wife and daughters you may read in the Holy Book." He finished delicately.

"The flying dream began with you holding a glass. Glass is made of sand and much sand is made by the cleansing ocean under the power of the moon. More important is the flying. One flies in dreams when the soul is on fire. Bathed in this great energy that allows you to sit so very straight and still perched on the very edge of your chair for such long discussions of these dreams, you left a desolate or chaotic place and flew over the cathedral. This holy building separated you from the man and he did not return. But the round object, dish or whatever it was that you gave up weakened you. Round is the shape of infinity and the source of strength. Once over the bridge that connected the two lands and bridged a vast and infinite void and you flew like a bird again. You had gone from strength to strength and were restored."

"I feel somehow, somehow, I could fly now if I could just remember the knack of it," she said.

"Many of us have felt that way. But we settle for flying in our minds and visiting in our dreams. And that is not at all an unpleasant thing to do. The next dream pitted you against a primal force. He had no skin, the membrane of separation that makes our life possible on the dry land. He was all muscle and bone and united without seam to the power he pitted against you. But your power, the power you flaunted when you flew above the tree tops, overcame him readily and you marched past him to a triumphal awakening. And that brings us to the last one. You know now the meaning of the black/red world and the demons prove it. You know something about the cave. Certainly if one were to enter the underworld a cave would be the place to cross such a border and certainly mankind has used the cave as a symbol of this dismal descent since ancient times. The turning machine may well be your own dream invention and the cartoon world that it turns you into is a strong metaphor for your real feeling toward this world, this world of space and time that our bodies inhabit. A soul such as yours that has curled back to the fetus in the hands of our creator and that walks the world encased in the will of His Holy Word may not see the value and urgency in this pale existence that we less buffered mortals ascribe to it.

"I will tell you a little secret if I may?" His voice whispered urgently as she nodded and almost held her breath. "As I age, I gain such a perspective more and more. In truth, it looks more like a cartoon world with each passing day. What on this earth, wise Sophia, do we humans find that is so intense and demanding? We spend our lives racing and fighting and competing for things that we probably would disdain if they actually came within our grasp. Would you agree with such a statement?"

Her smile was lovely and happy as she said, "I agree."

"And what color were the rabbits?"

"White," she said.

"And on that note we may adjourn. I to the comfort of rest; you to winnow what you have been given and to make it your own."

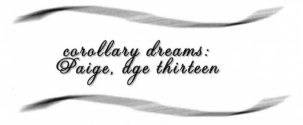

corollary dreams:
Paige, age thirteen

He was standing on a golden beach where all the sand was pure gold, looking eastward to the sea. Not too far from him a great golden city beckoned powerfully. The reflection of its fine gold caught in the cupped wavelets and shimmered almost to his feet in the fire of the noon sun. He carefully surveyed his path. The clear water before him was not deep nor did it seem to hide sea dangers. Reassured, he waded into the golden waters but his mother's voice telling him to come back brought him fully awake.

The second dream began on a square the size of a small town block that was surrounded by small shops. No roads led in or out of it. A rain started and he thought it came from heaven for it looked like a shower of gold, but when he examined it closely, it was small change in nickels and pennies. "Well," he shrugged, "if I can get enough of them I can buy something in one of the shops." But the asphalt was soft and they stuck; he could not pry them out.

Then he noticed a large, square wooden building that housed a spiral stairway standing open before him. A girl was waiting by the door to a ramp. She had brown hair and was slightly less than his height. She handed him three large rings with many keys on each. They walked up the spiral from staircase to staircase. He tried to open some of the doors that were next to the stairways but it was a very slow process of trial and error. He had to try many keys and frequently all three rings before he found the right one. A loud roaring shook the building announcing the advent of some large and dangerous creature followed by a crashing sound like the breaking down of doors. An intense fear shook his arms and rattled the key rings. Something was after him but he had to get the doors open; he could not run and there was no quicker way to find the right key. He woke up panicked and sweaty.

"The city of gold was beautiful?"

He smiled a half smile. "Yeah, it was. Extremely beautiful."

"Gold," murmured Dr. Zvee. "Gold—it is like the river. It is so rich and dense a symbol it comes to almost symbolize itself. As a yellow metal it is too noble to combine with any other element. So it is always brightly shining like the wisdom it personifies. It also symbolizes the mind or the intellect and the generative power that supports and stimulates it. Did you know there were two places in the body where sand is formed?"

"No," Paige said.

"Yes, two. In the head and in the lower body where generation takes place. How appropriate that this lower sand on which you stood be dream-mounted in gold. And would not the city be an appropriate and exciting symbol for the intellect?"

"Yeah, actually really exciting and really beautiful. It gleamed like a city of magic."

"Magic indeed! That city is waiting for you, Paige. You must only do as Goethe suggests in this short poem:
'That which from thy fathers hast inherited,
Acquire it! That it be thine.'
In fact you were going to acquire it when your mother, did you say, called you back?"

"It was Mom, all right. She always thinks I'm not ready to do things on my own."

"Or she may think you just need more time to harden and strengthen yourself before you attack. That city is not without formidable defenses and strong barriers. Let your wings dry a bit before you fly too high. The second dream is so full I am somewhat at a loss. Where should we begin?"

"I've got some questions. You want to answer them first? O.K. Why did the square surrounded by shops have no roads leading out?"

"This square was dream-formed to illustrate the actual state of your mind which is a square. The square mind form is applied to the surface of earth, for instance, to direct our measurements. The four directions are either at 90° or at 180° to it. You can see that both degrees are set in our mind squares. And it is surrounded by shops representing the minds, senses and sensations that you may walk into and perhaps even through to reach the world around you." He smiled. "It is not generally realized how closed into our heads we really are."

"Yeah. I've never thought of it that way either. Then why was it covered with asphalt?"

"You possibly already know that asphalt is made by processing petroleum, the residual of ancient trees. Your mind processes a mind sap symbolically similar to the tree product and this is what you actually saw covering that square. It catches ideas just as your square caught coins and it analyzes the worth of all of these. You found the sad truth that heaven was raining not gold but common coins for heaven is a common for us all. The gold, as we have mentioned, is reserved for another place. And now we come to that most singular square spiral staircase. You remember the six degrees of freedom, of course, and I have told you about the seventh, the spiral way in which we advance and learn within ourselves by spiraling up or down around our own spines?"

"Yes, I remember those very well."

"Did you connect them to this spiral stairway?"

"I thought they were connected."

"Very well. Then you met this young lady whose brown hair would seem to set her apart from you for you are quite blonde. But, she is not that different. At this moment she is your anima, your strength of the earth. She gives you three rings, one for your body, one for your mind and one for your soul. Each contains keys to unlock certain chambers in the physical, mental and spiritual world. With all these keys you were really confused. Too much too soon."

"Boy! Was I ever! I had the worst time trying to get even one door open. I guess that shows how hard it is to learn things."

"It certainly does and it shows you that there is even more to learning than you thought. You must find the information in its proper place and time and you must then correlate it and put it back into its place or into another place. The tyranny of position is surely upon you and that is the beginning of wisdom."

Paige thought on this for awhile before he asked. "And the roaring noise and breaking of doors?"

"These introduce the primal force and it tells you a great deal. First, it gives you an alternate way of dealing with those doors. You can simply use force to smash them down. Perhaps no other way will work. Second, it heralds the onset of a new power in your life. Can you clearly see now from the way your dream has set it up that everything in this dream is part of and inside you?"

"Yeah, I can see that. Puts a lot of pressure on me, doesn't it?"

"It does indeed because this force is one you must conquer and bring under your control. This is the work of the champion. This is what the wise king does. The champion forces that primal force to accept the intellectual commands of survival. You, Paige, are demanding that this force obey you, empower you and elevate your comprehension." He smiled. "Are you up to all this?"

"What are my options?"

Dr. Zvee chuckled. "Either you conquer it or it conquers you. But be of good hope. The force that roars at the doors is exactly equal to the force that resides in your mind. It is never an easy battle but it is always set up on exact balance. You are given an opponent that you can always subdue if you exert your absolute maximum effort." He laughed again. "What do you think?"

The tall, powerfully built young man snapped his fingers. "Just like that, Dr. Zvee, just like that." And he snapped them again. In the doctor's mind was the feeling that for this person it might be, "just like that."

corollary dreams in repetition: Sean, age twenty-four

These dreams began about age thirteen and stopped about age seventeen. They recurred as often as once a week. With each dream he was falling through large arches about ten feet high and six feet wide, which were of brick-gray color. The arches were spaced at roughly six foot intervals and were connected together by white walls. He could see clearly because of a very bright light far, far ahead of him where the arches began. Fear of hitting them was his only worry and it was quite a real possibility. Although the apertures were big enough to let him pass, he had no control and was tumbling over and over so he easily could hit one of them on some part of his body as he fell. The angle of approach to each arch had to be very precise. When he looked ahead, he could see the arches and walls gradually bending to his left.

On other nights about the same time, he dreamed of a great right hand. It looked like it was sixty or so feet away when he first saw it but then it would slowly but with great certainty move toward him. The hand was upright and held tautly open so it stretched slightly on its palmer surface as though it was clearly telling him, No! It was large enough that he could have sat comfortably on the web between the fingers. When it was close to him he would wake up.

About age eighteen a quite regular and enjoyable dream began that stopped when he was twenty-one. It was always in color; his other dreams were in dull tones of black, gray, white, and brown. He would take off from various wide-open-space locations flying quickly up into the air to survey the land and life below. This gave him a broad sense of absolute freedom and control and heightened his feeling of reality. He flew over fields and lakes and ponds and particular parts of the world's great cities that he had never seen before. Later, when he did visit them he often found vistas like the ones he had dream visualized and an odd sense of *déjà vu* gripped him, as though he had really been there.

"Do arches have any particular meaning for you?"

"None that I can think of."

"They are interesting structures. The word arch means old or ancient, as in the word archetype, and suggests you are falling back into your own past. It curves to your left, the direction of the spiritual world, to take you back to that world where your soul resides. You might think of this structure as a time machine tumbling you steadily toward your most ancient origins. No matter how we try we always move toward the future when we are awake, but in dreams this is often reversed. Not only do we tumble back in time but we can look at our own past by turning our heads. Another interesting part of this dream is your total lack of control. You may actually be wise enough to know this is a true state of affairs. The only real control we have over our lives is to change our attitudes. Does this sound reasonable?"

"Yes, certainly." Sean nodded.

"They span an interesting time period—when the greatest changes are taking place within you. So they recur until they have clearly demonstrated to you that you are changing and you are more and more coming to understand who you are and where you came from. But, what is that hand forbidding you to do?"

"I don't know. Do you think it is forbidding something?"

"What do you think?"

Sean was silent for some time. "I have thought about it many times and I really agree with you. It *is* telling me *not* to do something. I just don't know what it is I shouldn't do." He shook his head. "You don't have any idea?"

"Ideas will not help here. But your two masters, time and maturity, will one day make this clear to you. Give them opportunity to do their work and one day you will know. In the meantime, avoid even the hint of wrongdoing. If you are not comfortable with any action, avoid it!" Dr. Zvee looked at him closely. "Now tell me, is the flying dream a dream or a reality?"

"I really think they could be actual dream flights. Especially when I've visited those places later and had the really odd sense of having been there."

"Dreams are not always the ephemera we would ascribe to them, are they?"

"No. In fact, not at all."

*corollary dream of island and palm:
Tad Darnely, dreamed at age nine:
current age, nineteen*

He was on a small round island whose beaches raised it in the midst of a vast sea. A tall, thin tree whose branches started far up on the trunk was growing in its exact center. It was either a pine or a palm tree, he was not certain. Two men wanted to chop it down but Tad wanted it left alone.

"You may have heard that some dreams at this critical period dwell on fears of castration and this one could conceivably be so bent. But I rather doubt it. The dreams you have dreamed since then point to a deep, spiritual tide that nourishes your soul."

He paused for a question but Tad remained mute. "Island is male. A man is in the waters with his mother and with all other women as long as he is a child. But the ignition of the first pubescence acts to lift his intellect above the waters and root it into the deep earth. The flaming pituitary gland, controlled by his hypothalamus that uncycled when he was a bare three fetal months old, the continuous nerve signals, the continuous hormone drive establish his beach heads and set a bar of difference between him and all women, especially his mother. I am sure you have noticed how different men and women are."

"Yes, I certainly have. I tend to agree with Henry Higgins on that point."

"You agree that most women advocate change; most men like constancy, that the woman's great preoccupation is the home, that the man finds his identity as provider while the woman finds hers as the disperser?"

"Particularly as disperser. Have you ever watched women shop? They look like they're in a trance of ecstasy."

Dr. Zvee chuckled deep in his throat. "I believe it has been said that behind every successful man there is a woman making success necessary," and he chuckled again. "Once this island is firm enough to support the mentality, the dreamer then has the option of growing upward. Dreamers that dream Type-3 dreams do this and they guard that single tree that waves above their island's center."

"How do they guard it?"

"Mostly by hiding it. For in most men this growth is cut off, frequently by older relatives who are close to them—like their fathers. Those men who cannot grow into the spirit, fear it and look to stamp it out in others. Macho and want-to-be macho males belittle and denigrate the yearning to the intellect and the soul. You said the tree was tall and did not have branches until quite high up on its trunk?"

"Yes, that's how I remember it. But that was a number of years ago."

"Then the tree sounds more like a palm than a pine and a palm tree fits better. Palm is Tamar in Hebrew. It also means a pillar of smoke, a column or a pillar. That yearning, dreaming soul whose smoke billows upward in its longing fire as the glandular elements clash and intensify in their drive. And thus he grows toward the moon. You have had such a dream?"

"Yes, and I've been wanting to ask you about it."

"Next time, next time we have an opportunity for such a lovely afternoon we will speak of it again. You won't forget?"

"Never. I'll never forget!"

chapter three

alias woman of light

We can think of dreams as our mind's eye.
— Carl G. Jung

Thirty-three days of incarceration. One full month, plus three. A complete synodic cycle with three and one half days into the next. In a cell, six by six feet where two and one half feet of pacing space were taken up by a hard and rigid little bunk. Three gray concrete walls, one pierced by a small, barred window. The fourth was a wall of steel rods whose massively bolted door was the sum of her life interface. Thirty-three days of steel routine: up at six, breakfast of eggs and bacon, lunch at noon, dinner at six, lights out at ten. Thirty-three days of waiting, of grinding up carborundum time, sitting on that hard bunk, pacing, reading, looking out the barred window, talking to her mother, cooling her brain against the rage that could amount so easily at this hideous restraint. Thirty-three days of not letting herself think of where he was. Thirty-three days of staring against the interface of June Darnely.

Cardinal Mindszenty told us what happens to the self when wrapped in a cube of monotonous white walls. Not content to witness his pain, American scientists have set up an even more intense isolation—a diver's suit in a vat of still water. Here the very senses and body tensions that hook the mind to its dimensions are floated into non-function. In their sensory deprivation laboratories the stimulus-starved minds that could tolerate that lone-fear and lone-isolation for enough hours, literally wrapped themselves into themselves. They saw dreams, visions and violent sights as they journeyed and these they could catalog and document to their fellow scientists. But when they broke beyond the dream limbo they suffered their internal self-world with such personal intensity they could not later discuss *what* they had experienced nor *how* they had experienced it.

Napoleon's reaction was reported to be identical. While his army was occupying Egypt, he spent a night in the King's Chamber of the Great Pyramid of Giza. Emerging into the daylight the following morning his face was shocked and his manner timid, even shy, far different from the robust and confident soldier who had swaggered between those massive stones the night before. He refused to tell even his closest friends what had transpired under the pressure of those granite walls, claiming it was too intensely personal.

But none of these men could abide this state for more than a matter of hours, and every one of them could stop it on command. June abided it for thirty-three days with not the slightest shred of control or certainty of relief. She knew in fact that strong forces were bending the full power of their influence to make sure it would never end. Her lover was gone with not a word to mark out a day. Her family and home, the place where Robert Frost wrote "when you have to go there they have to take you in," had almost completed her expulsion. Only her mother came to her cell.

In this pale of incipient insanity her celestial soul groped out its canons of survival. It abandoned the all of itself and forgot who it was or had been. It forsook the hope that springboards from despair to despair. It humbled the fire and the passion of the deep June Darnely pride. It acted the automaton, the face and the stance of placid obedience to the will of her captors. June became an instant master of the vacant, self-deprecating, supplicating, and non-irritating smile.

Sleep came as it usually came, slowly, opening to the profound relief of reprieve; the hours to forget that self and its tiny cell and those thirty-three nights. She slipped deep into the peace of unconsciousness and hung on the sleeves of exhaustion—until the REM sleep pulled that fragile comfort away and she was forced to look at the dream that flowed ghoul-swift through her shattered foundations. To watch as the dream that was more than a dream burst on her attention.

Ten years were sliced away and she was sitting in the old car pressed in by her family; everything just as it was on the night she met the serpent that separated. A heavy night of no stars closed them in. There was barely enough light to shadow the dark and heavy pine forest they were going through, the old trees lightening and darkening as they were caught in the fast headlights. Will was driving fast and very intently. June studied the back of his neck where the muscles knotted under the press of his attention. Myrtle sat looking straight forward. Only the roar of the old motor broke the silence as even her brother's chatter was stilled. It must have been that the three had a pact—

whatever they had to do they wanted to get it done and over with in a hurry. Bumping and making sharp turns that alternately made her brother and her cling to the door handles or jammed them against the arm rests, brought them after a very long time high up on the mountain on a dirt-lonely road. The body slamming and roaring ceased as the car was braked to a fast stop.

His hands locked to the wheel and his body hunched and staring straight ahead, Will said in a hard, emotionless voice, "we are sorry, June, but we have poisoned you." June sat back as though he had slapped her. The voice was so cold and unfriendly.

"Yes," Myrtle affirmed, looking straight out the windshield, "we truly are sorry but it had to be done. This is the place we have selected for you to die. Get out! Now!" The steel command of her voice left no alternative and was exacerbating the pain in June's heart even as she opened the door, got clumsily outside of the car, and stood bent in supplication on the side of the road. The door barely missed her as it immediately slammed shut obviously pulled hard from the inside. The engine accelerated, gravel spun and flew, and the car whipped swiftly on up the mountain. A well of total isolation fell around her. Nor lights nor sounds broke through the thick darkness.

June stood stupefied and dazed, full of the wonder that possessed so much of her life. "Why? It makes no sense. Why are they killing me? What did they poison me with? Why, why, why? This is my family. These are the closest friends I have in this world. Why? Why? Why?" Questions were forming and bursting like popping surface bubbles and confusion was flushing out the thoughts of her head until there was no room for fear. Until she woke up.

She knew she was awake because the cell was exactly like she had seen it as she went to sleep and because she was not a child—she was eighteen years old and bulging of breasts and thighs. Even the book she had been reading to seduce sleep's forgetfulness was exactly where she had left it. But the room had been dark when she turned out the little ceiling light and now it was full of light. Now there was a room lighted with the full brilliance of fear.

It was a very bright light, very white, shading almost into the blue, and cold like death, like a hyper-charged full moon, radiating from a young woman stand-ing not far from June's bunk. The entire concrete cell with its steel barred door stood picked out in painful detail and even the hallway beyond the bars was brightly lit. She was the very source of emission of that light and in truth she was that light. And all the light, the light of the woman and the light that blinded off the steel and concrete walls was brilliant and like the purest of crystal; the steel bars threw dark shadows on the hallway floor. The woman looked directly at June who now raised herself up on her right elbow—the better to see and to study with the entire and focussed intent of her mind this being that stood in perfect calm and stillness.

She was exactly June's size. It was not at all like looking in a mirror: June was looking at June! This was a three-dimensional thing, exquisite and brilliant and solid in form, that had life. Her face was June's face and her face was a face of flesh. Her hair and June's hair were identical, shoulder length, parted and combed the same. June gasped in shock as she looked into the contours of her own identity.

She was very afraid with a growing terror and repeated aloud. "Go away! Go away! Go away!" But the Woman of Light only smiled; her mouth moved only to smile. She spoke in the language of thought saying that she understood that she knew June and knew her very well.

She repeatedly said: "All is well, be not afraid. All is well, be not afraid. Do not be afraid. Come and follow me and do not be afraid. Follow me. Follow me."

This perfect likeness wore a white robe that was neither flimsy nor transparent but was woven of white wool or linen with no pockets, no belt and no seams. A seamless garment that began just where her neck sloped to her shoulders hung to the floor, covering her feet in its smooth fall.

"Go away!" And again, "go away!" But the woman only smiled the lovely smile that arced the left of her mouth a little higher than her right and told June in soundless words that she understood and that all was well. That soft, gently seducing voice spoke into her mind and repeated her message.

"All is well. All is well. All is well."

June's desperation burgeoned and her terrors multiplied. She *had* to get *rid* of that thing! She began to look for something, anything, to throw at it. She pawed around her bed and table keeping her feet carefully off the floor while the woman continued to watch her and smile. June's hand found the book she had been reading; she clutched it and threw it in the same quick motion. She saw the pages fan out but it would not reach its target. When it touched the concrete near the woman's feet, at that very instant, the Woman of Light was eclipsed and the room overflowed with thick darkness.

Death crawled in that place and the horror of death riveted her to that hot bunk. She was sure she would die that night and in the heaving pain and terror finally gave herself up to its black embrace. But it did not come and the dark and the increasing horror of it got her up in that cave blackness, waving her hand around until she finally found the string that hung down from the small overhead light. That was the only light in that cell; there was no light switch. Its feeble glow was a candle compared to the violence that had just vanished. Terror and fright so possessed her that screams were jamming up into her throat, but some deep impulse forced her to hold them back and the effort was exceedingly painful. She paced back and forth and to and fro and around and around that tiny room in the heat of that stifling August night, kicking and re-kicking the thrown book. Finally she picked it up and put it back on her table. It was a Reader's Digest that either her mother or the matron had given to her.

From time to time she pounded on the door but no one heard her. Little by little she walked away bits of the fear that was shaking her body and shoving her heart into her throat. After a long while, after hundreds of trips around that claustrophobic room, she lay down. The lifeless dawn light was already filling into her room, bringing in another blistering day. In its harsh reality, she gained the will to shrug her shoulders and convince herself: what will be, will be, and sleep dropped heavily on her exhaustion.

Dr. Zvee thought for many minutes about that dream before he looked at her with a very serious expression and asked, "what is your impression of the dream?"

"I really have none. I had no idea what was going on in that tiny cell when it happened and I am no wiser now. But one thing, why did I throw a book at her?"

"She demanded an answer. Her presence demanded it. When you threw the book you told her you would follow the path of the book, the philosophical path, the path of the written word. Given that answer she turned within you."

"She was part of me?"

"Certainly. She was you."

June was anxious to get back to her earlier dream. "I should have started from the beginning. What did that dream mean that preceded the Woman of Light? Did the poison my parents gave me just mean that they killed me because I would not conform?"

Dr. Zvee chuckled. "So much to learn and so little time. But, we must take our questions in order. The real question you are asking is: why did you have the dream before you woke up to the image of yourself? And the answer is that visions of great portent are often preceded by very clear explanatory dreams. It is certainly possible that all of them are and we just do not find out all the facts. Certainly this one was. You were shown not only that your parents had rejected you, but that they had killed you in their hearts. I was just wondering if your little brother's face was painted in shades of glee?"

"He hated me, didn't he?"

"Yes, you were his Cain. It is not always the brother that kills the younger one forced by the pressures of survival. They then went on up the mountain through the pine or spine forest for a long distance and this distance is equivalent to time. From this, you may calculate how early in your life this expulsion had actually occurred.

"The poisoning takes place on the deep plane of your elements. You could say of course that it was a function of your nonconformity but that quite glosses over the real meaning. You were poisoned the moment the sperm invaded the egg. You had their intellect, their power of soul, their abilities. And these were not trivial. They blazed on your forehead like a shining mark. You may call it the Mark of Cain if you wish to be a bit theatrical. Only a mind of power, which was bred to that power, could stand the onslaught of the dreams you have known. But this power possessed you. It dys-controlled you. And they watched you, their juggernaut child, careen on the cliffs of destruction. Does any of this sound familiar?"

She shook her head slowly. "Oh my, oh my, but it's so true. How many times did my mother tell me when I'd stayed out all night or did some other thing that she disapproved of, 'June, you're exactly like your father!' And she'd stand there with her hands on her little hips as perky as a squirrel."

"You followed the star of your First Illusion until your dreams put it in perspective. Then you had to look beyond your death itself to find meanings for your life.

But this looking is for the well-hammered minds only. They further poisoned you by exposing you to the depths of religion before your mind was hardened and capable of supporting such thought. The final poison was planted by your brother. He saw your power and knew he had it not. He knew how deep the love ran in your mother that she would demand from you total responsibility and not from him. He drove you from them, from your will-less father and your guilty mother. The Serpent of Separation thrust in its venom at precisely that point. Would you not admit your brother was very adroit?"

"Oh, extremely adroit. He has it all and I'm out in the cold."

"Your mind, your soul, and your body are all neatly cut away from them as predicted by the Serpent of Separation and this is the poison they talk about in the pine forest. It will be small comfort to know that they and not you will bring it about but one day you will be completely alienated from your family."

"When I was thirty I would have argued with you, but not now. It has come about as the dreams suggest. Dreams are really rather terrifying! They really do predict our future! But, you said the Woman of Light was myself. Can you tell me more about that?"

"Seeing ourselves, Mrs. Darnely, is a very terrifying thing. Those who know of these things say it is the surest sign of our impending death. There were two deaths incipient in the cell that night: first you dreamed you were poisoned, then you saw yourself. You were quite right when you thought you were going to die. But a death need not *only* be a separation of the soul and body. In philosophy we speak of any change of state as a death. For instance, one dies to childhood to become an adult, one dies to sin to be saved, one dies to this world to gain that one. What *we* call death, the actual separation of the soul and body, is but one example of many such changes that occur as we age."

"I think I can see that now. Then I did die that night."

"Yes, relatively. You died to your parents, to your youth, and you took on the ill-fitting cloak of the adult. You died to your need of people and your life will be more and more alone. The robe the shining figure wore was the same as Joseph's coat of many colors. An alternate translation from the Hebrew is not a coat of many colors but a garment that reaches to the ground, and usually it refers to a seamless garment. John of Patmos saw an angel wearing such a garment and shining with light."

"I thought dreams were lit up by Now-Light. Why did she shine a light that varied with space and that cast shadows?"

"Because her Now-Light was gathered into her body and beamed from a specific point. That is perfectly possible with Now-Light."

"So, I saw myself and I was preserved."

"Just as Jacob saw the angel and his soul was preserved. He gained a new name because he wrestled with God and with man and he prevailed."

"This girl—was she a dream or a vision?"

"To be honest with you, Mrs. Darnely, there is no difference. It is a set of the mind, a condition of the glands, related even to the phases of the moon. When the mind is loosed for the revealing, the revealing will come in sleep or in waking. Remember Daniel's visions and how clearly he saw in the day. What you are really asking is: had there been anyone in the room with you would they have seen what you saw? My answer to this is, no. You saw in the eye of your mind and the reflections of your soul. Only you were privy to the events of that night. The Angels of Dreams are extremely circumspect about the wisdom they dispense. Only the dreamer sees it and only she may tell of it later." He assumed a slightly more comfortable position on his rigid chair. "You were actually offered death that night."

June shuddered. "You mean she intended to kill me?"

"What did she continually tell you?"

"She said: 'Come and follow me and do not be afraid. Follow me. Follow me.' Over and over."

"Do not be afraid and follow me! Where was she leading you?"

"I don't know. I really don't know. Where was she leading me?"

"She is your Daena, the alias who meets you at your death to guide you across the great waters. She was going to lead you home. To your spiritual home, Mrs. Darnely, to your spiritual home."

"So, if I had gone with her I would have died?"

"Certainly."

"But that's terrible! How could she do that?"

"Was it so terrible? Your fortunes had sunk to their absolute low. You were crossing that Jordan. Everyone had deserted you except your mother and even she certainly did not approve of what you did. Your future looked exceedingly grim. At that terrible moment your Daena offered you the solace of death and allowed you to make the choice. I do not feel that was so terrible. I think it was an act of pure charity and great kindness."

June thought long before she said, "it puts a different face on everything. It changes it all. What do I owe her then?"

"The best you can make of this life, the very best."

chapter four

emerald green with gold

What is the good man but a bad man's teacher?
What is a bad man but a good man's job?
If you don't understand this, you will get lost.
However intelligent you are, it is the great secret.
— Lao Tzu

The reasonable thing is to learn from those who can teach.
— Sophocles

June was standing with a crowd of people, all strangers with bland faces that blended into each other and left no hook to bring any of them to memory. She stood several feet away from a rather small stage, watching it intently. She could hear a woman offstage to her right weeping, then wailing, then intermittently screaming and crying in a loud voice in a most intense and inconsolable manner. This went on and on for a long time and still no one moved but all looked steadily at that stage, empty except for a classical old Roman-type lounge with the rolled arms at each end. It stood at the far left.

Suddenly, from the right of the stage a woman burst forth as abruptly as an erupting projectile. She bolted across to the Roman couch and threw herself face down while a very loud murmur of sympathy sounded in the audience. She was wearing a rather form fitting emerald green dress with gold threads running from top to bottom that June found extremely beautiful and interesting, a dress that covered her completely and extended full length to her ankles. She looked to be almost exactly June's size and her hair fell over her shoulders precisely as June's did then, covering most of the left side of her face.

June was shocked. Even the brief view, which showed only the left side of the woman's face as she ran, flashed an image of redness and swelling revealing that she had been the weeping one. The woman much resembled June in body and carriage. They were both about twenty-eight. June felt very close to her but had a strong sense that the rest of the audience didn't know or really care anything about the woman in spite of their loud murmur. The woman continued to weep and sob convulsively as though she had just undergone a great deal of pain.

June felt extremely sorry for her, extremely sorry and her heart was heavy with pity. Then she felt a powerful presence behind her and turned to look. A big man, a head above the crowd, massive of shoulders and arms, with a full brown beard, moving in steady power that no one wished to hinder, was heading toward the stage. But June knew he was coming for her. He was looking right at June and she moved immediately toward him. The crowd fell back and moved to give him room for he was a mighty scattering force intruding among them. When he was close enough and had cleared that space, he extended his right hand. She walked to him and took his right hand with her left hand. They walked toward the door.

June knew he would not harm her and she thought, "I will go with him anywhere. He will never hurt me." Then she woke to the deep night and her husband's heavy breathing.

"Was that you, Dr. Zvee?"

"It was your dream, Mrs. Darnely, so it is your decision."

"You mean I can decide if that man was you? How can that be? I mean either he was or he wasn't. How could my decision have anything to do with it?"

"In the world of dreams there is Dream-Truth. The dreamer decides on truth and this becomes the actual truth for that dream. The Angels of Dreams select, edit and send the dream but once sent it is all yours. Its truth or falseness, its relationship to your waking world, all this is under the pleasant domain of Dream-Truth. If you wish that man to be the same man as I, you need but tell your mind that it is so and Dream-Truth will seal it for you in granite. We really know this truth system rather well," a mischievous smile briefly touched his mouth, "and we apply it quite liberally to our non-dream reality. We make up our minds about the truth or non-truth of this or that in our world and what we decide becomes truth to us. Surprisingly enough, particularly if we are all agreed on some point, most of the time we get by rather well with these little detours from the absolute. Reality is more flexible than one might believe and the risk is small. If our manipulations of waking truth miscarry, we may look outrageously ridiculous but I suppose that does not hurt us too badly. Do you not find as I do that looking ridiculous is rather refreshing—especially when it is all over?" His smile broadened into a chuckle as she nodded agreement. Then his face set again to his serious thought. "But perhaps truth is too vast and too dangerous a word for our consideration of this sad lady of the green and gold."

She clicked her lips and tongue softly. "What I really want to know is: are you and the man in my dream my teachers?"

"Why is that so important to you?"

"I think, Dr. Zvee, when I understand *that* I will be far down the road of wisdom. Strangely enough, the East puts the greatest emphasis on the teacher/student relationship while the West all but ignores it. I tend to believe the East. So, I want to know: are you two my teachers?"

"If you say we are, we are."

"We're going around again. All I have to do is decide it and it's so. Frankly, Dr. Zvee, this smacks of a dream world." She stopped with a blush as "ridiculous" leered over her thought.

"Well?" There was a smug smile on his face.

She exhaled and sighed. "You're right. If the dreamer says it's so, her dream says it certainly is so. And I say you are my teacher." A quick bounce of her head added a "so there!"

"In all the years of your life, how many have you asked to be your teacher?"

"One—you."

"And you've told your dreams to how many?"

"One—you."

"Therefore—I am your teacher." He bowed slightly. "It always occurs in precisely this way. The teacher is but a student among many other students until the need of a true student marks him out as the special and only one to give her the time and direction for her teaching. Then he becomes her teacher. He can take other students, if he has the time and the need to teach, but she has only him. She can take students of her own but only her teacher will hear the confidences and build the logics of understanding for her mental progress."

"You said, 'true student.' What did you mean by that?"

"There are two general areas of teaching. A trade, a skill, a craft, a profession—everyone may teach some-thing—fall into the first teaching area. These are training drills to mold us into the image of our civilization and enable us to make a living. In America, we learn to be Americans by acquiring a certain level of expertise in our language, our literature, our measuring systems and by accepting our system of government and participating in it. To put it briefly, by doing all the necessary life acts in the American Manner. The same is true of all other countries.

"The second teaching area invades philosophy and examines virtue to impart the general and universal life principles. This instruction is not necessary for life. In fact it may interfere rather violently with the general processes we have described under our definition of life and most of us are far better off without it. Only the true student who asks the question: 'Where did I come from and where do I go?' is thereby put under iron necessity to seek such guid-ance, and will be given a teacher.

"The meeting is the ultimate experience: even being a teacher is nothing like meeting your own because the student's soul is on the line. This meeting we find as a theme in all the great books because it generates an explo-sion in the student's entire being that totally changes her life. There are no guarantees that all or even any questions will be answered nor would she ask for them." His voice stopped and he thought for a few minutes.

Then he said. "It is odd, isn't it, how some of us are bound and some of us are free. Have you ever read *A Dream of the Red Chamber?* No? It is a great classic. You know how wise the Chinese were, *are,* yes, even now. So wise. That book speaks of the binding of the soul to the soul in the world of heaven and how they find each other here in this world. The Kaballah says the task of The Holy One, Blessed Be He, is to spend much of His time uniting here on earth those souls that were united in heaven. From those come the perfect marriages. Soul mates, you might say. That is the mechanism.

"But I believe some of us are bound as teachers and students and that binding is equally firm—but totally intellectual. Souls that have nothing but this great love of beauty, eternity and virtue in common, even among these there is a recognition, and it is an instant recognition. The student recognizes the teacher by great need, even if the teacher does not immediately recognize the student. And the student pursues the teacher and demands, yes demands this teaching." His fist smacked into his open hand with a loud snap that made her jump. "And the teaching will be given. Whether the teacher wishes it or not, makes no difference. Vivekananda writes that whenever a true student arises a teacher will be given to her. And there will be one for you." He gazed at her. His face had softened even a little as he looked. "Even if it be one as ancient as I."

"Age has nothing to do with it. I'm convinced of that," she said.

"You are quite correct, of course. The teacher of the second teaching is bound by much more rigid criteria than age. He teaches with his life and the stories of his life and therefore his life *must* be impeccable. This is mandatory. The goal of the second teaching is to equip the student for self-recognition that she find her genetic and intellectual peers and comes to study the glass that reflects the deep principle foundations underpinning her life. Thus she becomes comfortable on her world path." He smiled at her. "It sounds like a tall order, as they say."

"Yes indeed. I seem to take all the risks, but that's fine. With you as *my* teacher I'm sure, Dr. Zvee, that I can't go wrong. And you will go with me anywhere. 'I will never hurt you,' you said."

He replied, "that is the attitude of the true student. You know you must face much unpleasantness to find the knowledge you seek and you know you must make a total commitment to the path leading to that knowledge."

She smiled helplessly and shrugged her shoulders. "What choice do I have?"

"None, absolutely none. When stern necessity is laid upon you . . . ," his voice trailed off into this old thought until he caught himself, "I had no choice either. But you have come to hear of this dream and there is much to say. Emerald green is her dress and green is the color of the herb. There is a very strange place in the Bible. It says in Genesis that God has given every greenness of herb for food. Listen to those strange words! Not the herb itself but the greenness of the herb is given for food. And green is the very color of chlorophyll that transforms sunlight into organic food for all the life on earth. Do you not see that we eat the very energy of green when we eat the plant? It is that wavelength embodied in our lettuce that nourishes and feeds us. We are eating greenness, precisely as Moses tells us!" And his voice rose in triumph at the thought.

"And the dress. It is shot through with gold thread that runs vertically from her neck to her feet. This gold spins out and dazzles through the First Illusion. The gold that symbolizes the intellect threaded through the life skein that is suffused with that greenness and swims in this Veil of Life. This is the intellect that biases and makes secure the life as we know it. For it overcomes the chance that haphazardly now saves and now destroys life. And this intellect is nothing but the command to survive, the very basis of the command to be fruitful and multiply that is built into our genes and chromosomes. No, it is deeper than that. It is built into the DNA and RNA of which they are made. It is the insatiable desire of these two molecules to reproduce themselves that makes life insist on surviving. This is the fluff of the First Illusion and it makes Technicolor meaning of the whirl of planets and the basically mindless and dull, very dull, birth-growth-reproduction-death that we have defined as life for our species."

"Is there a reason for the gold thread running in the dress the way it does?"

"Indeed there is. All these threads run vertically. A thread has only length, lacking breadth and width. It is a rather accurate simulacrum of a dimension. So the gold threads hint to us of a stretching that pulled the head of June Darnely's alias above her sphere, arched her like El Greco arched his saints. Freed to one dimension she whirls and rotates. If she can whirl with sufficient spiritual velocity she can peek over and beyond that black body radiation and see. My, my. What indeed did that lady see? Did her crying change?"

"Yes. When she was behind the curtain she cried and screamed and wailed like an Irish banshee and very loudly. It sounded like one in acute pain who was being tortured or undergoing surgery without anesthesia. When she lay prone on the couch with her hair veiling most of her face she moaned as though exhausted from an ecstasy of torment."

"You accept that she was you?"

"I accept that."

"You grieved for her and for yourself and a loss that you could not recoup. Your life at that time was filled with anguish."

"I don't understand it. My husband and I had such a close and even exciting relationship—until I got pregnant. I was in my eighth month and horribly fat and bloated and unattractive. He was so good to me and seemed to be enjoying that thought of the approaching fatherhood so much and then the dream came. The day he told me about it he was angry and he said. 'That kid is killing you! Damn it, June, that kid is killing you!' He had seen me in my casket surrounded by candles and the baby in a smaller casket next to me. He turned from me at that moment. My life became a misery of running to my folks, and you already know what that was like, and running back to him and trying, trying, trying to bring him to see that we had too much between us to throw away."

"He could not see that?"

"Not at all. Time made it worse and even worse."

"Did he have other such dreams?"

"Not that I know of."

"That is most odd." He stroked his beard slowly. "He reversed roles with you and he became the dreamer but he could not live with what he saw. He began to separate from you until the marriage was forced to end in divorce. He saw much but he understood none of it."

"What did he see, Dr. Zvee?"

"To not go astray, let us clearly distinguish sides. I always feel a bit self-conscious when I talk of sides as Duchamp dismissed them as an impression of the air that one leaves on the room in his passing. But sides are more important than this sardonic Frenchman would admit. The action began on your right. But to the woman in the green dress it was quite reversed. She wailed the many hours of her banshee woes from her far left. When she came out she ran to the couch on her right. Is this clear to you?"

"Yes, it's clear now. She was I, not my mirror image."

"Precisely. And the time behind the curtain was much longer than you would imagine. She went in there early in her pregnancy and stayed for eight years." His voice rose. "No wonder you thought it a long time before she emerged. You can see also that she ran across the stage to keep some continuity between those times. Now! What did your husband really see in his dream?"

"I don't know." She barely whispered this, so taut were her throat muscles.

"He saw the great lathe of non-being and he saw his wife loaded between the dead centers and he saw the slow chisel of Aaron diminishing you to accord with Procrustean Laws. He saw the pregnancy of impossibility, for two bodies cannot exist in the same place at the same time, subliming you, de-liming you back to the state of the child. You had sundered the veil and walked brazenly in where the old gods speak, where the rhapsody sutures your brain to your soul and that spirit. Your strength was level to that tremendous achievement. And he knew you. He knew the slender grasp its base dimensions had upon your mind. When the lathe had completed the work of a lathe he anticipated your transition. A woman of death were you to him. All this he saw among the candles."

"I had no idea he was so perceptive. My brother must have been tuned into what was going on then also. He had a dream about the same time. He said he was standing on a loading dock watching freight being taken off an ocean liner. One of the pieces was a large and beautiful Egyptian style casket. When he went up to it he saw it was open and I was lying there dressed like an Egyptian and dead. Suddenly I sat up and even years later he told me how I frightened him when I suddenly came alive."

"Some are wise beyond their knowledge. They understand more than they can articulate. Your husband and to a lesser extent your brother are proving to be such men. Your husband particularly is also a man who demands of the sensual to mark up the days of his life into meanings of the First Illusion. He will cling to this even to the moment of death. He can never follow you, never peek among the tombs to watch the macabre dance out the new image. When you came back from the fast turning Eden, laced toe to neck in the fine spun ovarian gold, he could not follow and he was forced to draw it to a climax. He knew what was in the pregnancy for you; the same thing precisely that your Egyptian coffin portended. Both of them drained out your gypsum and you were, 'e' which equals out of, gypsum, but another term for calcium. You in turn threw yourself prone on the old Roman *klinus*, to shield your newborn and the seat of your will from the power that unhooked you. For that was the last time he would look into your eyes. One day you may look up clinoid process and see that the pituitary gland rests on it." He added almost as an afterthought. "And you did not lose your edge."

"Does this have anything to do with the bearded man?"

"Madam, it has everything to do with the bearded man. He was there to witness, to see the chilling and cylindrical evidence that marked you a true student. Now he accepts his student."

From his erect and rigid position in his straight chair, his beard flowing uncombed about his face into the balding circle about his head, he gave a marvelously accurate imitation of one who passed his judgments from Olympian heights. Visibly shaken, June Darnely leaned her chin in her hands and studied the patterns in the oriental rug. Gradually her strength returned and she stood up. He stood with her. She desperately wanted to embrace him, to hold this great old oak in her arms and let his massive power sublime away the throbbing of her heart. But he did not encourage such familiarities. When he bid her good day at the door he shook her right hand and pressed it between both of his and even that embarrassed him.

June continued to run to her folks and back to Tibor.

corollary dream of the greatest teachers: Sophia, age fifteen

Sophia was walking in a field with her religion class but they paid little attention to her or she to them. Her teacher was also a vague figure as this woman was busy with the other students. Behind them was the ocean and a golden, gleaming field was in front of them with grass about waist high. They were walking idly around and decided they had to accomplish something. Setting themselves to this task, they began to study the Bible every day. When they finished each chapter they moved farther away from the ocean and farther into the field. There was no light or darkness to mark them, she just knew that days were passing and they were advancing in their knowledge.

By the time they finished the last chapter of Revelation they came to a white wall she knew to be limestone. It was four to five feet high and about two feet thick. From this wall came forth three men with the usual height and appearance of men, about thirty years old, with white faces and dressed in monk's robes. One robe was white, one blue, the other saffron. These men moved among them and were talking to them, probably about life and its challenges and how the champion brings these under control. One of them seemed to be Jesus. She could touch them and feel their hands and arms and chests. The hands felt like light and their touch was warm and gentle. The three men put out their hands together to show them and they thought they had the glory to see the ocean again. All the students jumped over the wall to view the accomplishments of those study days. What a privilege to see the glory of the waters through their hands.

"Do you remember what the man you thought was Jesus was wearing?"

"I'm not sure."

"Think about it and if you can remember, let me know. It would be very interesting. Does this dream mean anything to you?"

"Not much I fear."

"Then let us take it from the beginning. You started with the ocean behind you. If you think of it, you will see that the great water is always behind us land-based creatures and the land is always in front. When we study, we make progress on land just as you did and that progress is measured by our distance from the ocean. The field, golden or not, is that which marks our progress. The moment the Lord God made the beasts of the field, there was a surface to measure against. But study always meets a wall. There is a time when we cannot go further. Either we have learned all there is to know or our minds will not encompass the subject. And your wall was limestone. What is limestone composed of?"

"Calcium."

"Precisely. The same element we have in our bodies?"

"The same as our bones."

"Yes, indeed, and the way our nerves speak to each other. You came to the bones. At first your ocean was at your back. Could you not say it was behind your backbone?"

'Yes, I guess it was. Does the backbone always separate us from the waters?"

"I believe so. But look now what your dream did! How interesting that it should have turned it all around for you. First your ocean was behind you, then you came to the limestone wall and it was in front of you. Very well thought out for a dream, do you not agree?"

"Yes, well, yes, I think so. So now when the men showed us the ocean, they were pointing beyond our backs and yet we were facing forward?" Her voice rose in the difficulty of such belief. She shook her head. "But, who were these three men?"

"This is a rather difficult concept. When you are older, Sophia, it will be easier. We will leave it for awhile and pursue your question. I would believe they were the same as those that became transfigured. Take that Bible please, and read Matthew, 17:1-3."

"'And after six days Jesus taketh Peter, James and John his brother, and bringeth them up into a high mountain apart, And was transfigured before them: and his face did shine as the sun, and his raiment was white as the light. And, behold, there appeared unto them Moses and Elias talking with him.'"

"How about that, my wise friend? Does that answer your question? Now, I have another for you. Why three different robe colors?" She shrugged and shook her head. "No idea? Well, white contains all colors and is the proper symbol for infinite potential. It is also the color of purity. Blue is heavenly or celestial and certainly is appropriate for such men while saffron is the color of the robes the Buddhist neophytes wear. This is a combination of red and yellow, a constant reminder to them to bond their emotions with the power of discipline and abstinence. One more question. Would any other study than that of religion have led you to the limestone wall? May I answer that for you?

"Only this study bring us to the confrontation with the boundary of ourselves and with that within ourselves that jumps our vision beyond ourselves to the vast expanse of that infinite sea."

chapter five

self vs self

Dreams are the royal road to the unconscious mind.
— Freud

It was the middle of winter, a particularly cold snow-storm was blasting out of the north, but weather was never a considered factor in June's trips. She said good-bye to her family, drove out of town and started southeast. The snow was blowing heavily, radio warnings were out, there were no other cars going or coming, so it was an event when she was passed by a big diesel. At the next cafe where she stopped for coffee, a man approached her table. "Are you driving that little blue and white Chevy?"

"Yes, I guess I'm the one in the Chevy." He was a man of good size, stout and muscular. Everybody else was bundled up but he was wearing only a heavy shirt with the neck open and sleeves cut off at the elbows. A fuzz of black hair showed above the V-shirt line. His head hair was the same, black and curly and seemed to fly around his face like a mane. He was one very tough looking man, tough like a grizzly bear, and fear caught her as he stood close to her table. But his manner was so mild and the storm so bad, she relaxed. She needed all the help she could get this night.

"This is a rough night to be out, young lady. People have been killed this night. Where you going?" She told him. "Well, there's nothin' more ahead than more of this. You finish your coffee and leave ahead of me. I'm gonna pass you down the way and you probably can't keep up, but you stop at the next coffee place where you see my truck. You come on in there."

It worked out the way he said. He barreled past her but at the next island of lights, there he was. She pulled in and he came over to her car. The heavy snow didn't faze him. "A woman got killed tonight. Her throat was cut with glass. You go on in and have something. I need to check on Baby. That's Baby," he said proudly as he pointed to his truck. "I never turn her off. She just sits there and parks and waits for me." June went in but he totally ignored her; sat with two state troopers and talked. After a while he nodded for her to go. They made many stops during the night and at one of them he told her to drive over to the service station, she had a headlight out.

A serviceman came out. The grizzly man checked the right light and explained what was needed. Soon a box was handed over and he asked the price. When he heard it, he stepped up closer to the serviceman and said, "don't tell me that. What do ya think you're pullin'? I know what these lamps go for." He asked June for the money for the knocked-down price and she handed it to him. As the truck driver replaced the light she watched him bending over the car, hair blowing in the wind, bare arms steadily working. He never looked up. When the light worked again he told her to drive back to the cafe and go in and get some coffee.

All night they leap frogged from truck stop to truck stop until they reached the junction where she had to turn south. He stopped his rig and walked over to her car. "I'm goin' on to Chicago. It's not so bad now and it's daylight. Get a motel and get some sleep. You should be O.K." He walked back to his truck and swung up into the cab.

June waited long enough to fold her hands, bend her head and say, "thank you, dear God, for that wonderful man. A man that looked like a grizzly bear got me through this night. Thank you, dear God." Then she laid her head on the steering wheel and fell into a deep sleep. When she woke she could not tell if it had been a dream or a reality. She drove south through steadily improving weather.

She was in the air in the total darkness of that night, unrelieved by stars or moon. She could not see the land nor any mark to certify her location. Yet there was enough light to see the grisly occupation and opponent that demanded her ultimate strength. She knew without being told this was a live or die contest: a desperate wrestling with another person who was equal to her in size and power. Not strange this equality, for when she looked it was herself she strove against. She was as twins and complete between the two of them: two women at their fighting prime of twenty-nine years and exactly equal in every other way, tearing and flaying the skin off of each other. Already their faces and arms were stripped and the red muscles exposed in their violent contractions but there was no bloodshed. The battle was intense. Her strength was actually increasing but her counter-self waxed as she did. It was a grim and intense fight and dealing death by ripping disintegration the rage of their goal. A seething was in June's heart. She was being attacked and she wanted to retaliate fully in return for her injury. The flesh and its underlying fat was ripping off in greater and wider strips under the flash of their frantic fingernails.

She awoke panting with the exertion, more tired than when she had gone to bed but wired, intensely aware and claustrophobic in that bed. Black coffee in the dark of the prefabricated kitchen calmed her nerves slowly as she carefully felt herself for areas of skin loss.

She sighed deeply in her tension. "What a miserable way to spend the night. Why can't I just sleep like sane people do?" Her heart throbbed and ran at a high beat as she looked at the hot, black liquid and blessed its bitterness. For she was still full of the anger that drove her fingers into the other flesh.

He got up and led her by the arm into the warm old aroma of the book-lined room where a marble statue not more than six inches high sat on the central table. It was a copy of the classical work showing two wrestlers. They were dressed in boxer or wrestler shorts and one had an arm lock on the other.

"Now, tell me, Mrs. Darnely, what is so interesting about these two men?" She looked from different sides as she walked about it but could not see anything at all obvious.

"Look closely! Very closely!" He encouraged. Finally, she admitted that it was an interesting statue of two wrestlers but that was all she could see. With a theatrical sweep of his hand he picked it up and held it so she could see both men's faces at once.

"Look! Do you see? The faces are the same! They're identical!" His voice rose in register and volume.

"Why yes, you're right! You're exactly right. Their faces are identical."

Then he chuckled. "You see, there have been other great dreamers in the past and one of them carved this statue." They returned to their seats. "What do you think of that, Mrs. Darnely?"

"Oh, I, uh, well, yes, I see now. That man is wrestling with himself just as I was wrestling in the dream with myself. Yes, very interesting." And she tried to sound like it really was interesting, her face blushing with the effort.

Dr. Zvee laughed heartily. "Do not feel badly if you do not immediately understand it. It appears very simple, yet it is the most difficult, and possibly the most important dream you have had. Certainly, it is one of the most widely applicable. For it tells us what we may know of the champion and what it requires to attain that grade. The dream is so powerful the concept it carries reaches the level of truth. I call it the truth of Self vs Self." He stopped talking and stared ahead of himself. "I will tell you something. Do you know that I tremble when I approach truth?"

"Well, no, I didn't know. I would think you would be very relieved to find it, for truth is a very good thing. I mean, it is the best thing that is." Her voice tapered off in the pained look on his face.

He sighed deeply. "That certainly is the commonly held opinion. But, it gives me little comfort. That which is absolutely true, that which is eternal—makes our souls tremble and we dare not approach it. While that which is of this world and changes in the mouth of everyone who speaks—blinds and confuses us and hamstrings our governments. And that which is truth in our world is but half truth at best."

"Why do you say half truth?"

"Because our world is a world of two. Two because two is the number of separation and we are forever separated from the Eternal World. Two because we must have two of everything to function in this world. Two because what is true for one half of us struggling souls is false for the other. Is it not the demand for this twoness that drives us into marriage, that slight pause between 'I do' and divorce?"

"Ah me, how true. Cynical, but true."

He chuckled. "Possibly less cynical than true—and there we are, back to truth again. You may clearly see, Mrs. Darnely, that all truths are not created equal nor are all men created equal—in spite of that odd phrase in our constitution."

"You're referring to the place where it says, 'We hold these truths to be self-evident that all men are created equal?'"

"Yes."

"This is not a truth, then."

"Do you know any men, women or children who are equal? Even identical twins are not equal."

"But doesn't everyone just assume they mean equal before the law?"

"Such an assumption is indeed generally made so we quietly admit that there are truths and there are truths and that this is a terribly difficult area. Can you not see, there are great ringing truths glowing around our holy places, terrifying our souls in their Divine power as they bring His sublime majesty to our earth? And that there are humble truths cowering like Cinderella among the ashes? We deal with these humble ones. When we find one this truth entrains us to live in accordance. This is perhaps the only real evidence we have that we are dealing with truth. Ben Franklin alluded to its difficult nature when he said that most of us, when tripping over it, pick ourselves up and go on as though nothing had happened.

"The truth of the Self vs Self is a humble one and yet it is an absolute one. Every human must fight it or suffer the consequences. There is much about it that is thoroughly unpleasant. Well do I remember the first time I encountered

it and the young man who said: 'Remember, he who conquers himself is greater than he who conquers a city.' I too
was young then and you know how the young will spring at
any subject long before they have studied it. Well—knowing
nothing about conquering myself and having read a lot
about conquering cities—I was prepared to do battle over
this broad and deceptively simple phrase. I am so pleased
that I was not given a chance to make myself ridiculous."

He stopped talking to allow her time to order her
thoughts. "Do you want any more discouraging words on
truth?" She shook her head. "Very well, then, can you tell
me anything else about your dream?"

"Even as I was wrestling and exerting all that energy
and feeling my skin being torn off in great strips, I was
thinking how strange it was that I felt no pain. In fact, I
couldn't feel it at all. I couldn't even feel her touching me.
Is that characteristic of most dreams?"

"I believe it is. We usually just see our dreams.
When the other senses become involved the dreams
change and come much closer to our waking reality. And
that was the only observation you made?"

"Yes."

"Do you see that we really only fight one battle and
that is a lifetime affair?"

"No, I don't see that. We fight many battles." Her
voice was more assertive than she intended.

He seemed not to notice. "It would certainly seem
so. And yet—let us consider. When we compete in any manner and for any stakes—everything else being equal—who is
going to win? The one who has the most training and discipline or the one with the least?"

"Well, of course, the one with the most training
and discipline."

"Are these easily acquired or are they difficult to
acquire?"

"Quite difficult."

"Could we say that acquiring them is a battle?"

She thought long on this before she admitted. "Yes, I see where you're coming from. If we don't fight the battle of Self vs Self inside ourselves we will surely lose the next wrestling match. There seems to be some humble truth in what that minister said."

"Are you willing to admit that already?"

"Well, I'm willing to consider it. If you're right, we do fight only one battle, the battle of the Self vs Self. But how about a king or a general? They don't fight directly. They fight through their soldiers. They don't need, use, or fight the Self vs Self battle."

"Certainly they do not fight directly, but they must lead their men. Is that not so?" He looked at her from the corner of his eyes. "Are all kings successful leaders?"

"Well, no. I can think of a few that were dismal failures."

"Ah," he said as he turned the full force of his gaze on her. "So what, Mrs. Darnely, makes a successful leader?" She made a few starts at it until he said. "Perhaps it would shorten our discourse if I encapsulated it for you. Can you not see that the king can only lead his troops by the example he sets. He must be at least equal to his men in training and discipline."

"No other method will work?"

"No other method will work. Physical strength, willingness to bear pain, chastity, cheerfulness and acceptance of hardships are his lot." He sighed and smiled. "Unfortunately, there is no place for love in war, but I am told by those authorities on marriage that the opposite is quite prevalent."

She laughed with him. "As one who is at least an authority by virtue of having failed twice, I most sincerely agree. There is plenty of war in love. "

"And how does one gain the patience and wisdom to acquire these difficult characteristics?"

"The Self vs Self." She finally admitted very softly.

"Do you mean to tell me that all of this was in the dream where you saw yourself fighting this very battle of Self vs Self?"

She shook her head slowly. "It's amazing that I didn't see it before but all of it was, indeed, in my dream."

"Perhaps you will also agree that war is not the only battleground of Self vs Self. Look around us. There are hundreds of misshapen and bulging humans literally eating themselves to death. Their bodies are slabs of fat, their rudimentary muscles allow their joints to grind away their cartilage and their brains are shrunken from obsessive television. Just a moment away from Altzheimer's disease."

"I can think of hardly anybody I know who isn't this way. They need so badly the discipline to work and study and trim their bodies and firm their minds and fill their souls."

"Well put, Mrs. Darnely, well put. Are you familiar with the words, 'Take no thought of the morrow for the evil thereof is sufficient.'"

"No, they are new to me. Is that from the New Testament?"

"Yes. Can you see by substituting 'evil' for the word, 'good', the writer has put the thought very neatly into the Self vs Self mold? These humans have learned to look for challenge and welcome the battle to control themselves. In the Orient, the yogis have named the selves. That which is more accessible is the Atman, the one we must first control. Beyond the Atman is the Ishvara, and this brings us deeply into the realm of spirit. Or would you rather stay with the champion?"

"I think the champion is an inexhaustible subject. Let's stay with it. And before you can ask me I'm going to ask you: who is the champion?"

He laughed with pleasure at her quick perception

for he certainly was going to ask her exactly that. "I define the champion as one who fights and continues to fight the Self vs Self battle. And here the emphasis must be on the continuing to fight. At one time or another we all fight ourselves. But we grow tired or discouraged and give in on first this point and then that one until we are no longer fighting at all. This struggle is a lifetime battle. We must never stop. The champion is the one who never stops. Would you take that Bible and read Matthew 24:13?"

"'But he that shall endure unto the end, the same shall be saved.'"

"Now if you would be so kind as to read Mark 13:13?"

"'And ye shall be hated of all *men* for my name's sake: but he that shall endure unto the end, the same shall be saved.'"

"Jesus thought so much of this concept that *two* of his chroniclers included it in their books in almost identical language. Now, can you see the champion clearly?"

"Quite clearly, I think. Can you tell me some of the specific battles of the Self vs Self?"

"Certainly. One vast area is the appetite. We do not fight the appetite and we do not accept hunger as our daily bread. We over-eat and do not exercise and we grow fat and fall into the grave of obesity. Surely this is death. Another area is our desire for sex. Watch those around you as the mania to procreation takes over and renders their minds impotent. For a meaningless shudder in the loins the most important plans are put aside and the best brains are lost. Today there is AIDS and the greater and greater certainty that anyone who is promiscuous will become infected by it. Yet it seems to be of least concern to those who should be most concerned. The self you fight is an image of your body that your mind must constantly face. This assures the fulfillment of your bodily needs because this image is adorned with the most luscious and desirable rewards.

Everything possible is done to guarantee survival of the body. Are you your body?"

"No," she said firmly. "Not at all. I am not that. I am something else. I am *in* my body but I am not *of* it. A stranger. A sojourner. A temporary traveler on this globe and then it is all done."

"Would you agree that it is more necessary today than ever before to fight the self?"

"I guess I don't know. It seems like it's always been necessary."

"Mankind has been warned not to remove the consequences from the sin and this is exactly what we have done. The outstanding example of this is the development of penicillin, which quickly spawned a vast family of drugs even more powerful. Smoking, alcohol imbibing, excess eating; all of these would have taken their toll and we would today realize how deadly they are and we would limit their use. But with these 'wonder drugs' we can be as frivolous as we wish and not suffer the consequences. We live in a strange world, Mrs. Darnely, very strange. Man and his ability to turn nature against herself has taken over our fragile skim of life here on Earth and all is being set awry."

"Where will it end, Dr. Zvee?"

"I shudder to think about it. Indeed, Mrs. Darnely, I shudder to even think about it."

chapter six

snow grip: church of fire: steeple of desire

*Children come through their parents, art through the
artists, and dreams through the dreamers:
Children, art and dreams are always different from, and
usually greater than, their medium of transmission.*

The trip going was not bad. Even Rabbit Ears Pass
was comfortably dry and she sped over it and spent a
week with her parents. It was decided that Tad

would stay there over the holidays and June would take their Christmas gift back with her to Tennessee, a forty-inch screen TV.

"You know, June, there's storm warnings to the east. Don't you think you ought to wait a day or two?" her father asked.

"No, Dad, no. I'll be all right. You just take care of Tad. I can make it back just fine."

She started out early the next morning in her little blue and white Chevy coupe. The only place for the TV was on the seat next to her and it was so big she could not reach around it nor over it. As her father put it in place he carefully locked the door. "There you are. It should ride all right and you're locked in. Now you should be safe." No low-life was going to get into his daughter's car.

The drive went all right. It was cold and snowy, but no great problems until she started up Rabbit Ears Pass. She had no chains and no money to buy any. The road there is steep and the pile of new snow made it glass slick. Near the top she lost traction as she slowed for a curve that swung to the right, felt her little car whine to a stop as its wheels spun helplessly, then start to slide back and to the left. There was a drop-off with neither rails nor rocks: nothing but a straight fall far to the valley below. June looked with helpless desperation as her car reached the left edge; then she looked down into empty space.

"What a way to go," she said aloud and wondered what it would feel like as she bounced down the mountain. She was so close to the edge, if she opened her door and stepped out she would drop into empty space. She could not get out and her car was still sliding to the left. At that instant she felt a hard bump and looked back to see a four door Nash Rambler snugged up to her right rear bumper. Her car had stopped. The driver's face was frozen in fear as he looked at her. He could not get out on *his* driver's side, so he had to slide across and open his passenger door.

Approaching the Chevy's right side, he yelled. "Get out!"

June yelled back. "I can't."

He approached and tried to open her door. "Open this door then and I'll help you out."

"I can't." She simply could not reach around the big box to unlock the door. She explained this to him.

He kept looking back at his car, the fear expression increasing. "You've got to get out. My brakes aren't good and could go any minute. If they go, you go. I saw you sliding and was just able to snug up behind you and stop you from going over. But you've gotta get outa there. Wait here a minute and I'll get a tire tool and break the window." By now two more cars had stopped on the right side of the road and were watching this drama develop. Just as the man was about to go back to his Nash for his tire tool, a snowplow came up. The driver got well ahead of her, looped a chain around her front bumper and pulled her to the top of the pass. There he stopped, released the chain and came to her window. He was very irritated.

"You got no business being out here in this snow without chains. You got any idea how close you came to going over that cliff? If that Nash hadn't come up just when it did, you'd be dead. Now listen! The moment you get to the next town you buy yourself a set of chains and when it's snowing don't ever attempt this or any other pass without them." He shook his head. "You don't know how close you just came. I tell, you, lady, your left tires were half way over that drop-off." June shuddered. "Well, get moving, but get those chains!" He waved her on.

When she woke there was still thick darkness in the room. Tibor's heavy breathing of deep sleep close beside her was the only sound besides the rumble of the furnace. She was filled with an unusual and ominous sense of unreality and she said over and over, "you are June Darnely. You are thirty years old, you are married to Tibor

Darnely," until something of the firm feeling of herself came back. She closed her eyes and played it over and over. "Funny," she said softly to herself, "I'm not sure if the church was on fire or if it was a church of fire. But who ever heard of a church of fire? Maybe there was." She remembered reading about primitives that worshiped fire and vaguely wondered if there was some such foolish meaning in her dream. But there was never anybody to talk to and wonder was of so little value.

She was walking in a strange city alone at night but it wasn't completely strange. She and Tibor had driven through several new cities to get to their apartment and there was something vaguely reminiscent of them in the skyline. She walked in a very nice residential district on a wide and smooth concrete sidewalk, moving along steadily on the right side of the street. The sky was black, without a moon, but there was plenty of light for walking, more like twilight than night darkness, ample light to show her the tall buildings on the skyline and the mass of houses around her.

A soft, masculine voice with a gently molded southern accent reached her from behind and said, "Beware! There is a fire in this city. Be very careful."

She looked around to find the source of this voice. A very tall square church with high steeple that towered above all the other buildings was burning with a bright yellow flame that licked against the sky. It must have been of wood, old and very dry, for the tower of flames roared up beyond her sight. As the sparks of fire fell back to the earth, she could see they would fall on her. Fear possessed her as she realized she could not get away. "My God, will these things burn me?"

A sudden shift of the wind brought a rain of fire that fell thick about her, drenching her head and face. To her great surprise, it did not burn, nor was it hot. It felt cool and looked white and shiny and wet, and was slippery when she slid her hand over it. She was surprised that it did not hurt her and even more amazed that the church kept burning in its great thundering plumes of yellow fire and was not consumed.

"How can that be? How is this possible?" Then the darkness of that little bedroom replaced the bright fire. She looked at Tibor's back for awhile, and got up.

"Had you ever heard the voice before?"

"It could have been my father's voice. But I'm not sure."

"And you were not aware of the fire until the voice warned you?"

"No, not at all. Then I turned and there it was blazing behind me and the church burned and it burned and it didn't burn up. It was still standing."

"Have you thought of what a church is?"

"A holy place. A temple. A house of God." She shrugged.

"It is also an interface between us and infinity or non-being or even between us and God. Does one go forward to God or back to Him?"

"I've never thought of it, but, I suppose. I suppose we go back to Him. We read of our return to Him, going back to Him. Is He behind us then?"

"Where was your church?"

"Behind me."

He sat back and looked smug for a moment while she went over the argument.

"If God and infinity and all are behind me, what's in front?"

"At this moment everything in front of you is exactly the space between us, for behind me is also infinity."

"And a burning church?"

He laughed. "Well questioned, Madam, well questioned."

"So if the church is behind me all I need do is turn

around." June said.

"It is time we addressed this question. When you turn around in your dreams you turn from this world back to that one. If you turn now while you are awake you will not turn in your body, you will turn with your body and your world will turn with you. Your face defines your front."

"I see. Even if I'm alone I always face forward. How do I turn as I did in that dream?"

"It takes great meditation and for Castaneda it took three women. He had to develop the 'Second Face of the Warrior' and that required a turning within his own head. He literally looked out his own back."

"When I turn in my dreams I do the same thing? I turn in my head? So I looked out my back to see the church burning?"

"Quite correct. You turned and saw what was always behind you. You saw the yellow flames, the lemon and canary flames of infinity roaring up from the church and it was not consumed. Is it obvious now that such flames burn forever and never consume the object on which they sit?"

"Like the burning bush?"

"Exactly like the burning bush. The effluvia of such a conflagration is not hurtful. It is a balm that heals. 'Is there balm in Gilead?' asks the prophet. And now you know there is indeed balm in Gilead."

"I've heard the church was made in the pattern of man?"

"Indeed that is true. One enters from the east and passes the altar where sacrifices are made. Then through the nave—and is that not very reminiscent of the body of a ship?—to the Holy of Holies where only the high priest goes to the furthest limits of the west. The tower for the bells and the steeple were added later. The great bells that toll the times and the seasons as the body tells the times and the seasons."

He combed the twisted fibers of his beard with his fingernail before he spoke. "A strange city. That does bring up many possibilities. It is not likely that you would see a church burning in a familiar place. No, you must go to a place of strangeness to see this." He chuckled and said, "Oh my," and, "*tres difficile*," a number of times before he continued. "This is a place that would be strange to you. Do you remember, by any chance, what Cabell said about church steeples in *Jurgen*?"

It was her turn to laugh. "Yes, indeed. Believe it or not, I have read that book. And about the little devil clinging to the church steeple. Do you mean that a steeple could refer to something like that?"

"Well," said Dr. Zvee, "Cabell alluded to this, and, he certainly may be right, and, while we cannot say he is wrong, on the other hand . . ."

". . . she had a wart." June finished the statement for him, delighted to prove she had really read the book.

"Particularly when the fire was cool and white and wet," he added.

"Is it a church on fire or is it a church of fire? Men have worshiped fire from ancient times. Did they have churches that blazed and were not consumed?"

"When their dreamers of dreams dreamed on *this* dream they understood. The fire gave life to the church and burned in the church. The fire flamed above the apostles' heads when they spoke in tongues and the fire burns on your forehead when the yearning becomes over-great and bids you home. They did not need a building that we call church. Three small fires kindled on a mountaintop to catch the first rays of the bright and new sun served the worshipers of the Vedas as fire enough and church enough. They had the vital essence of church flaming before them. The roaring fire that rushed up from the place below and chimneyed out the sushumna, as the yogis call it, into the right hemisphere, that heat welded them to non-being that started the flowering from the Tree of Knowing Good and Evil and sealed them into consciousness."

"All of that in the citron flames?"

"Wisely asked, Mrs. Darnely, wisely asked. Indeed, all of that was in the yellow flames."

"But wouldn't we be wiser to worship the fire which is the real energy of the church? The ancients did and they seem to have been a lot smarter than we are."

"We would be wiser to worship the fire as the first principle of our faith if we thoroughly understood that the fire we worship is but a simulacrum of the true fire you saw in your dream. We could worship the sun if we understood that it is but a symbol of the Ancient and Sublime God Head that is behind it and controls all things. It is so easy to become confused between the real and eternal and the unreal and temporal. Having fumbled around this question for a million years and having nothing better to show than our present mode of worship, it is probably wiser for us to continue as we are. Those who dream and can understand what they dream, those few and selected souls, we may allow to worship as the spirit may move them. Do you agree?"

"Yes," she said reluctantly. "I suppose." And she frowned her disappointment most charmingly.

chapter seven

a world that goes to sea

She was in the engine room of a great ship. Everything down there was a bright white and blue and charged with the rumbling-throb of the great power plant that ran the ship. It was all exceedingly bright. She noticed many young sailors going about their business all wearing bright white and blue uniforms. They did not see her, or if they did, they ignored her. Presently a very big man stood in front of her. He had a great white beard and white hair but was neither bent nor feeble.

They looked at each other for a few seconds and he

asked, "would you like to go up on deck and scan the sea?"

She answered, "Yes." He asked the same question a second and third time. She answered the same. He directed her to the steel circular stairs and told her that when she was up on deck, if she would turn her head, she would see a pair of oars in case she wanted to use them. Up on deck she did see the two oars in a kind of cross at her head level attached to the ship. She walked on and saw the ship was of great size. Every part of it was a brilliant white and blue and all was very bright. The light came from nowhere and from everywhere. There were no shadows, not even in the corners. It obviously did not come from any artificial light nor from any sun. She liked this light very much. She was thinking how comfortable she was, not too warm or too cold. She looked out over the bright, bright sea. It was a deep blue with a little white here and there. She could see a great distance. She woke up with a happy and comfortable feeling.

"And how are you this evening, Dr. Zvee?"

"Better, Mrs. Darnely, better now that you're here. Did you decide who the man was?"

"I want him to be you. Yes, he must be you. And since dreams deal in Dream-Truths and this is my dream and I control that truth, he is you." She bounced her head briefly for emphasis.

"And that settles that question."

She grinned. "That's what you told me. But why did you ask me three times if I wanted to go up on deck?"

"Because it is possible to go up on deck with your mind, your soul, or your body, or with all three. You said, yes, to each question so you wanted to ascend the winding stairs all of a piece. You wanted to leave the depths of your source of power and begin to plot the course you are to follow. And there was another reason. Do you remember how old you were then?"

"Why, yes, I was thirty-three."

"And the three is a play or a duplication or a multiplication on that thirty-three."

"Do dreams do that to us? I should not like them if they got too deeply into mathematics. The world is very pleasant without a great deal of mathematics."

He laughed. "You do not realize that mathematics makes the feet firm so they will not slip."

"Well," she huffed, "there are certainly other ways of doing it than getting mixed up with math. And why a ship?"

"The ship is the symbol of the world of life or it may symbolize just mankind's journey on the infinite waters. How many times does the ship come into play when one is searching for the eternal? Jonah took ship from Joppa and was washed overboard. Paul went by ship. The early Christians had small ships hanging in the catacombs. Even some of our words like naval and navel identify the self and the ship. Also the ship symbolizes the church. Is not the main area of the church called the nave? This symbol is further amplified in the sailors who are moving about. Each of these may represent a person of the world, or a cell of your body, doing what it must to make all the activities of your life possible. White is the color of potentiality. Your ship has a great way to go before it will become what it can become. Blue is celestial or mental and it shows that you are bound to the path that will take you away from the First Illusion and directly into the second, exactly as your separation dreams indicated. The oars are your arms and they are crossed in your non-doing. At this moment you are doing nothing: it is all being done for you by the big man and by the sailors. The cross also represents the holy cross that you will take up when you separate from the river. But that is in the future."

"That light around that ship fascinated me. It was without shadows."

"We agreed dreams occur in Now-Time. That is

the light of Now-Time that we may call Now-Light. The light of eternity does not beam from one place. It floods from an infinite number of sources at the same instant of Now. So this Now-Light is distinguished from daylight which has only one source. Your Lady of Light was a notable exception."

"What you're saying about Now is that Now does not exist here. Now is in eternity and we see it because our minds can view eternity."

"That is quite perfect. In our time/dimensional world only past and future are possible. To know or even think of Now, our minds must be of eternity. And, they are!"

"I've heard that we are really sparks of God."

"Yes. We all are sparks of our Deity. Or, as Mark Tobey put it: 'We are all waves of the same sea.'"

chapter eight

value and the search for it

S he was walking on the left side of one assigned as her guide, a golden blonde boy of twelve dressed in light yellow, loose fitting garments. She was thinking how similar they were, how close to him she felt, and yet she was a full twenty-two years his senior. They were in a lovely meadow, green and lush, moving along together in the slow comfort of a warm day. Far away they could hear a faint humming and stopped to listen. As it grew fainter, they walked on until they came to a lake. This was almost perfectly round and small enough that she could easily see across it. A large tree or log extended from the bank to the middle of the water. No words flowed between them for none were necessary. Thought and instantaneous comprehension did it perfectly. She knew she was to walk out on that log, that she must face whatever waited in the middle of the lake and act accordingly. She found the path solid and steady and had no problem keeping her balance.

Not until she was close to the middle did she see a black figure that quickly resolved itself into a priest wearing a long black robe that fell to his feet. His black hair was tonsured as a monk and the starkly contrasting white face compelled her attention. She was not sure if he was standing on the end of the log or simply on the water. He indicated with a crook of his finger that she was to come and stand before him.

A slight bow with his hands to his sides. "Good morrow, Stranger. Thy prayer has been attended in lofty halls and the Virgin of Lakes speeds thy course. Oh thrice fortunate! Thy guide in the fullness of his good wisdom hath aided thee to this, *thy* holy place." He pointed to the crystal clear water. "Here is thy cave and all herein is thine: the jeweled sword and another treasure of even greater worth that I dare not name. Yes, they are thine and thine alone. Go and claim thy patronage!"

She studied the water. Clearly could she see the cave. Even allowing for the shortening of distance by refraction, it was not over six fathoms and she was a strong swimmer. There was no doubt she could reach the cave easily. "But then," she wondered, "with the weight of the sword and whatever else I have to carry, will I be able to get back on the log?" Death by drowning was a death by terror. She looked at the priest whose eyebrows were massing in anger at her hesitation and that further flamed her fear. Then she stepped back, shook her head to tell him, "no," and turned away from his frustration.

"When the wayfaring one will not claim her heritage, what is a poor priest to do? How many eons must I stand?" he wailed. She walked back over the log where the little one was waiting.

Again, she heard the hum. It was getting steadily louder now, loud enough to frighten her. They looked up and scanned the sky. Finally, a tiny black dot that slowly gained size was seen moving near to the horizon. Eventually it got close enough that she could make it out to be a great black serpent with enormous wings: for it too had flown too close to the great heats. The hum was reaching a level of discomfort and it throbbed in her body like a froth of desperate fear. Images of love, pictures of calm, assurances that this giant creature would never harm her, that she should be still in her soul and unafraid for, indeed, that serpent loved her, flowed from the mind of her guide. And suddenly she was soothed and quieted. With a great roar like a legion of hummingbirds the serpent flew down and slithered around and around her body in a great circle, rubbing her back, caressing her spine just below her neck. For the first time ever in a dream, she could actually feel this rubbing. And it was this that drew her slowly into wakefulness where the feeling persisted. She bore it all the day and it was marvelously comforting.

The second dream opened on a bright moonlit night. She suddenly flew from the ground to the top of an ancient castle made of gray rock, and landed on the foot-wide sill of a high window. She could easily stand upright on it and look over beautiful green, cultivated fields with carefully spaced trees. A wide moat gleamed like a liquid band of silver below her. She glanced inside. The window was the only opening into a room at least twelve by twelve feet square.

She laughed to herself and said, "with no door the

only way back is to fly and *I* can do that." While looking back out the window, she heard a man's laughter behind her. She turned and saw in the darkness of the far wall a man lounging on a rock bench. She walked to the center of the room.

He was still laughing and said to her, "got drunk tonight and flew up here. I couldn't have flown up here if I hadn't been drunk." He laughed again, "now how am I going to get out of here?" And his laughter was abrasive and hollow.

She thought, "well, that's your problem," walked back to the window, admired the view, stepped off and was sitting up in bed.

Dr. Zvee slowly shook his head as the pieces of the dream marched steadily into order. "It is just too much. It is too great. Where does one begin with such a plethora of images? I suppose we may as well dispose of the most pressing question: should you or should you not have gone to the cave? Certainly, the priest thought you should and was very perturbed when you backed away. But he has eons to wait before another will come who is entitled to these jewels. And only the entitled may claim them." He looked at her and waited for questions that did not surface.

"There are two dangers, Mrs. Darnely. The first is that you will not be able to come up. You may run short of oxygen or your body be overburdened with fatigue and unable to swim. Perhaps the lake is actually deeper than it looks. Or the treasures may be too heavy for you to carry and you would not be able to surface with them and have to make the terrible decision between death and riches.

"The second danger is that you will not want to come up, for here illusions blend their greatest magic. How calm and sublime is the bottom of the lake. How at peace would you be! One dares such a delight only if one is truly prepared to spend eternity there. The second dream illustrates these points. The man who became intoxicated and flew to that inaccessible room, what would become of him?"

"I don't know for he lacked the power of flight."

"And what was your opinion of him?"

"I felt sorry for him but I guess the real truth is that I felt superior to him. That is bad, isn't it?"

"Bad or just truthful? Which is it?"

She thought on this for a while. "Maybe just truthful. For he had foolishly gotten himself into that room and had no way of getting out."

"You on the other hand were quite capable of flying out. You were doing that which was in your power. He had usurped power. He had found in the power of alcohol the ability to fly. Like artists who sear their minds on drugs, these souls can get in, but never again can they get out. The road into hell is broad and inviting but no road leads back to this world. However majestic that room may have been, death is too great a price to pay for it. Observe it well, Mrs. Darnely, for there is a wide lesson here. Do not reach for those things in this or in that world that are beyond your strength. It was wise of you to leave the treasures in the cave and bring yourself back to the solid realities of this life. If you are to have such things, they will be within your power. If they are not, avoid them.

He continued, "how often do we see those around us trying to break through to the spirit energies and succeeding only in muddying their lives? The prophets that lived to tell us of that world waited until infinity, that hunter of men, found them and forced them to the experience. Do you see this clearly? I ask a rhetorical question for I know that you know and understand this, as it is your dream that illustrates it so perfectly."

She nodded. "Yes, I understand. Go only so far from the strength of your own life as you must go to save your own life and the lives that depend upon you." She moved to a more comfortable position. "But, tell me if you will, more about this cave dream."

"In its landscape scenes, scenario, and general plot, this is the classic hero story. Had you gone down into the lake you would have retraced the path of Ishtar, Sinbad, Tannhauser, Odysseus, and a thousand other heroes with a thousand different faces as Joseph Campbell said. What you found there, how long you stayed, and how you later described it would have been the basis of a new and modern mythos. Remember, it was a Chinese emperor who said, 'I have descended into the well and brought up the naked music and set it in order before you.' In this context, the dragon is especially interesting. The Chinese say the snake swims free in the waters of eternity until it finds the flaming pearl. Then it takes it in its mouth and becomes the dragon. Did you notice whether the animal had a round object in its mouth?"

"No. I don't remember that."

"Have you read about dragons?"

"Not very much."

"They really symbolize those scholars of the very great learning. When a Chinese official retires to a mountain retreat to meditate, he is said to be a sleeping dragon. He is expected to come back and put his wisdom at the service of his state.

"You thought the boy guide was twelve years old. Could you elaborate on this?"

"Twelve is a very critical number for this dream. Twelve is the power of the soul and that is the power that is leading you. Your soul sets the stage and directs that action. You know all the uses of twelve such as the months in a year, the synodic cycle of the moon, the twelve signs in the zodiac, and the many places in the great books. I need not elaborate further on this. Twelve, then, sets the stage for a dream that is under the power of the soul, one that emerges from the right hemisphere.

"And he walks on your right. Since you are the dreamer and this is all taking place in your head, he is stimulating your right hemisphere directly so you perceive no words; only images. He is so close to you and you are to each other that no words are necessary; it is instant communication. This is the point, Broca's and Wernicke's areas, where the gods still speak even today and used to speak continually to command mankind. Did you think of this young man as a lesser god? If so, you were not too far wrong. He was attached at the very cell where the soul is attached. Is that not where one addresses the Tree of Life?

"With his golden blonde hair he is a creature of the light, of this world, of the supernal moment. He is the antithesis of the priest and all that stands behind him. He guides purely by his great wisdom in the light-world. The priest, on the other hand, controls the path to the underworld. His robe is black for he has burned it in the fires of eternity and it ever smells of the fumes of that place. He has taken what is at his feet and put it at his head.

"The hum you heard comes from two sources; one is the beating of atoms on the ear drum that one hears in intensely quite rooms; the other is the hum from the engines of eternity. You may remember that Shakespeare mentions such a sound hovering over the island in *A Midsummer Night's Dream.* Joyce says, 'I hear the sound of many waters far below.' Some great artists hear this sound. At first it terrifies them but then they accustom themselves to it and put it to great use when they seek to build those special works that will be called their masterpieces. It guides them through the creative process and puts everything in order for the culminating work.

"In the middle of this lush meadow, which is to say at the very middle of two dimensional life itself, your two dimensional life, lies the lake. We do not often think of it but our lives are really lived in only two dimensions. We see, feel, navigate and map the two dimensional surface of earth. Only because of our eyes and brain do we see the third dimension and this is the one we use like a safety rope to escape this world.

"Water is symbolic of those primal waters below the firmament that were parted on the second day and gathered into seas on the third. One of these seas is gathered at our back. Do you remember what we said about the river?" She nodded in agreement. "That is the place where the waters have gathered. That is a sacred place. These waters certainly may hide a cave that holds the gold and the treasure and they are the only path to it. We need strong swimmers. The log of wood; have you thought about that?"

"I wondered if that log going out over the water had a meaning similar to that of the Trojan Horse?"

His eyes widened and he said, "I think you are correct. When we divorce all of the emotional brouhaha from the wooden horse, it is but a means of entering Troy, even if it did topple the topless towers of Ilium. Wood grew on the third day of creation and since almost anything may be made of wood, it is considered the same as primary matter; anything may indeed be made of primary matter.

"At the risk of being redundant, I should like to elaborate on the figure of the priest. This man who has devoted himself to eternity and wears the burned black robes that extend to his feet is an important being. He has black robes as we said . . ."

". . . because he has gone into the realm of the great fires and has been burned by them."

"Exactly. He has literally become his robes, for he is himself burned away just as Cinderella, the soul burned to a cinder, is scorched away and only her name remains. To stand as he stands on that pond, he has given up all that is of this earth and all that is of desire. Burned black with longing he is no longer seared by it. Just as Alcibiades' father lost it when he aged. This priest is your border guard, letting only those who have paid the price into that lake. You have paid the price. In Roman legends he is Pluto.

"The jeweled sword is Excaliber, a sword of absolutely unopposable power. In the German legends it is called Nothung but is not described as jeweled. It took the Anglo-Saxons to encrust it. Who wields that sword is the victor in all battles. If it is taken, the hero who takes it conquers. This is the sharp, two-edged sword that comes from the mouth of the angel whom John of Patmos saw and described in Revelation. Are you anxious to conquer the world?"

She laughed. "Not at all. I am quite content to watch while others make a hash of it."

"Then you were right not to risk that dive. One dives for the sword *only* if one must conquer in the world, in the intellect, or in the spirit. It is not given for all of us to so conquer. Some, even many, have taken that sword and ended up as dead as Siegmund.

"Dreams have many levels of interpretation. On the surface your refusal to go into the pond means you have given up marital ways and wedded joys and turned your back on such pleasures. Having done so you now will live alone and even be creative. If you have recently or at that time been involved in a decision concerning love or marriage, you can see that the dream advises against it. Love is a down going for the jewels and an uncertain returning.

"You walk back to the meadow, to the lush field of life, and there the winged serpent comes to you. It swims through the upper waters and flies around you, encompassing you, comforting you, and assuring you that the separation from the pond was a good thing." He chuckled. "The Serpent of Separation returns. But this serpent loves you and rubs your back, the place where the second infinity ends. You could not know it at the time but in retrospect it is clear; it was his counsel that encouraged you to avoid the attachment that you would have formed with the lake. Also, it is your intellect and your understanding that has taken wings with the energies released by no longer going into the pond. On one level this flying serpent is your brain and spinal cord.

"The priest's disappointment is not a concern to you. You neither succeed nor fail this task but you act as your nature and as your goal demands. Your goal is not to be a Hamlet, as Eliot says, but an attendant lord, perhaps.

"I have been much interested in the three dimensions lately and see something of them in this dream. These dimensions are the most universal ideas in our world but they do not exist in reality. There is no place where they are kept nor is there any materiality to them. They are pure mental constructions. I first thought of them while I was studying Genesis. You are undoubtedly aware that God made the heavens and the earth in six days. Have you thought that the first three days each added a dimension? The first dimension on the first day, second on the second. Then, on the third day He caused to spring forth from the earth grass, herb seeding seed, and tree of fruit whose seed is in it. I think these three forms of plant life are quite clearly a rehash of the three dimensions, the tree obviously being the vertical one. This dream of yours throws some interesting light on them. You were walking on two dimensions over the pleasant meadow and fields. Then you went out on the log, which we can visualize as one dimension, signifying that your act was taking you out of our time/dimensional world. You refused to dive into the pond, which would have carried you along another single dimension, the third or perpendicular one. So, you refused to fathom the lake. You stayed in the world of two dimensions, but your serpent of eternity flew down to you along that third dimension." He looked at her anxiously. "Does all this make sense?"

"I think I'll have to study it much, much more before it will come easily."

"Is it interesting?"

"Oh, extremely so."

He laughed. "My verbosity reminds me of Kant. When Dali read Kant he found him totally opaque. But he hammered away at his work for he felt that anything as dull and difficult as the works of Emanuel Kant must come from the pen of a genius." And she joined in his laughter.

corollary dream of searching for value: Tad Darnely: age twenty-four

He dreamed he was gliding on a flat disc about four feet wide over an arid and desert land full of holes that were being dug by about thirty men with wolves' heads. They knew what they were looking for but Tad didn't. He came back and skimmed over this place four or five times. When he returned for the final time and landed they were all assembled in a group looking at him. He realized that they had found what they were looking for but he didn't know what they found. One of the wolf-men dropped down on all fours and came to sit by his left side.

"The human with an animal head or an animal with a human head: the searching soul assumes an animal head or an animal body when it stoops to enter the over-soul. This is one of the meanings of the Garden of Eden. If this dreamer takes what is at his feet and puts it at his head he becomes like an Egyptian god and has the characteristics of animal and man. Or he might be a monster like the minotaur born from the union of Minos' wife and Zeus. Or he might separate from his animal body and realize how different he is from that, and that would make him a sphinx. Either way the beings that are digging are more than the sum of man and beast. They have crossed over. Another interesting example is the mermaid. This is the soul that has gone back to its elemental sea and given up all claim to its maleness. Once in the waters it is a female. But, what are they searching for? Do you have any idea?"

"I really don't know." Tad said. "I would suspect gold. Gold is associated with the desert. And gold would be the ultimate as it is also the symbol of the intellect. What about that disc I'm standing on?"

"It moved of itself in the dream?"

"Yes."

"It is a symbol of eternity and the infinite power of eternity. The round shape is perfect for eternity as the square shape is for our world. It is the same as a flying carpet. But the crux of this dream is to know what they are looking for. Remember these are your animals: one of them came and sat by your left side. You sent them out in the beginning as phantasms from your right hemisphere. You were prospecting with them. I believe you came to find true spiritual gold."

desert transformations

S he was in a land she had never seen before, in a severe desert country where nothing but the whistling sand and shifting dunes were there to leave no mark upon the landscape and run off to the horizon. A woman appeared at her elbow carrying a very young child on her left arm. She wore a rather large scarf or something similar to it, perhaps a bandana, on her head and this hung down and covered part of the baby's face. She wore a very colorful, loose fitting dress, held at the waist with a rope belt that fell to her feet. She was a very pleasant looking person, the same height and age as June. She handed June the ring that she was holding in her hand. It was a large heavy ring, as a man would wear.

"This is a ring that belonged to you ages and ages ago. You wore it when you were nineteen and it is of great value. At that time it was the gateway to Germany."

"Good heavens," June said. "That was twenty-two years ago. I really am getting old."

The ring's appearance accorded with the woman's statements. It was well worn, quite old, made of silver and set a sphinx of lapis lazuli.

The woman moved away and vanished into the landscape. The ring was no longer in June's hand, and worse, she had no idea of how to find her. June walked aimlessly until she came to a small cubical house of rough lumber or wooden poles painted with thick layers of gray paint. Through the entrance set in the middle of the front wall June could see dimly into the dark room. It seemed quite bare except for the woman who was now sitting in the middle of the room in the Lotus position.

June was very irritated and asked in a loud voice, "why did you take my ring?"

"I didn't take your ring!" insisted the woman. She immediately got up and stretched out her closed hand, dropping a rather heavy object into June's palm. This new ring was quite different from the original.

It was very delicately and accurately made, all of gold, depicting a serpent bent into a circle with its tail in its mouth. One gossamer and very finely worked gold wing fanned out from the spine of this snake. Admiring it and trying it on convinced June that it could only be worn on the fifth finger. That wing got in the way if any other finger was used.

The woman smiled and moved into the darkness of the cube building. June left the ring on her fifth finger, looked up and suddenly she was outside in the desert again and far from that house. On the ground, she saw two serpents. They were also of gold, very bright gold, and shot bright rays all about them as they coiled around and about each other. The woman had returned by then and they looked at the serpents together.

June smiled with her. "I know they can be dangerous but they will not harm me. I have a great deal of confidence that these two snakes will not harm me."

"Do you see any difference between this dream and the ones we have discussed up to this point?" Dr. Zvee asked.

She sat up straight for a few moments and frowned with concentration. "I really don't see a lot of difference between them."

"You do not see that this dream that takes place on the burning sands of the desert is a dream ruled by your intellect? That everything, with the possible exception of the woman's movements, moved according to the laws of the waking world?"

"Well." She looked at his face for awhile, measuring her thought against it.

"I would say that you were facing a very important decision that you were going to make with your intellect." He widened his eyes into questions.

"Yes, that is true. Actually, I was being pursued into marriage by a very persistent man some years my junior. I really wouldn't have thought of marrying him. But, well, the flattery of a young man finding me attractive after my rejection by Tibor, and the fact that living alone is not the most delightful state, when he came to my home and actually begged me to marry him—I finally gave in. If he hadn't done that I would have gone my way and forgotten about him. You said I was making this decision with my intellect. I thought all our decisions were made with our intellects."

"No, Mrs. Darnely, no, quite to the contrary. The

vast majority of our decisions are not made at all but simply follow our needs and wants and most of the rest are emotionally derived. Some, indeed, are intellectual. Taking a business partner, starting a business, what to eat, and many others that you may add, are all intellectual decisions and should be made in the left hemisphere. Even the decision to marry is intellectually summated in many societies where it is handled by those not involved. Parents, marriage brokers, and agents of this sort arrange them. In America we wish to marry for love and when love is vibrating between the partners there is no hesitation in the decision. It is made in the vat of pure emotion and springs directly from the right hemisphere. It is well said that we should consult our hearts before we fall in love, marry, or do any act that passes for emotion in our lives. But, instead of heart, let us think of right hemisphere."

"Would you explain the hemispheres and what they do. I keep getting them mixed up."

"An excellent text that draws together the work of Roger Sperry and the scientists who gave us the split-brain work, and adds a fascinating dimension of literacy, is the *Origin of Consciousness and the Breakdown of the Bicameral Mind* by Julian Jaynes. Have you read it?"

"Yes, but I still keep getting them mixed up."

"Perhaps if we started from the real beginning it would allow you a better grasp on these ideas. When God was creating He had not one but two tasks: first, to preserve the individual at least until it was mature enough to procreate, and second, to make procreation so attractive the individual would take the necessary risks to preserve the species. The mixing of DNA and RNA is a highly self-risking business at best, so He set aside a lot of intellectual power toward this end. We may define the intellect as that process that allows an individual to survive. From virus to human, the best constructed physically and mentally have the best chance of survival: we say these individuals are the most intelligent in their species. It has become so refined in us that we can out-think many possible reasons for our individual extinction and anticipate them. In other words, Mrs. Darnely, we can get the better of chance. We can bias chance. We can load the dice in the exact way that augurs most auspiciously for our survival.

"All you need to do is think of penicillin. Do you realize that the average human life span has grown from forty-three to over eighty years since it was invented? If you realize the truth of this, you can clearly see how violently we have biased chance and stacked the deck in our favor. And penicillin is only one example."

"This bias is relegated to our left hemispheres where we know who we are, where we can reason syllogistically and where we can access our memory banks with a marvelous device called self-consciousness to learn from the past, be productive in the present, and plan for the future. Since we are the only animals on earth that can do this, we naturally dominate our environment."

"This is astounding. I never realized that we were so powerful. So all the decisions that influence the survival of one of us come from the left or logical hemisphere?"

"Exactly correct. And it turns out that the best environment for the intellect is dryness. And that Mrs. Darnely, is precisely why you went to the desert with the problem at hand."

"Can we call the right hemisphere a jungle?"

"Certainly. Or better still, an ocean, the great wombing seas where life began and where it burgeons—and where it is very wet. This is the origin of emotion and passion that drive us to procreate. Fortunately, we have all the power of the left hemisphere watching out for us when we do this. So, we choose generally safe areas for the exchange of our DNA."

June giggled. "So we have a dry side and a wet side; an intellectual side and a sexy side." She giggled some more.

Dr. Zvee blushed slightly and said in a dry voice. "It might be more appropriate to call the right hemisphere the creative side. You can see how nicely it follows that our sexual creations and all other creations such as art, music, literature, spring from the right side." And then he had to chuckle a bit as she was still giggling. "And this gives proper credit to testosterone, which is our truly creative and truly destructive hormone. Can you not see that the entire earth has been built and over-built in the name of human procreation? For when the right hemisphere is not busy painting brilliant images to lure us to bed, it is painting images to lure us into theaters and art galleries and symphonies, any number of soul seducing sights and sounds. Now, shall we replay your dream?"

"Oh yes. Please do," and June's voice caught with excitement.

"You met the woman in the desert who has a silver ring set with a blue sphinx. This is of some value and you used to own it. Would it be too bizarre to say that this woman is from your right side?"

"I thought she was from my left. Didn't you say this was an intellectual dream?"

"I said the dream was intellectual so the mode of operation will be analytical. But that does not mean that every actor in it will be of the left side. If we consider that the woman appears and disappears, has her child and then does not, perhaps we should place her on the right. But on the other hand, does Germany have special meaning for you?"

"Certainly. Tibor and I spent our first married year there and conceived our son there."

"You would agree that the ring was the key to Germany?"

"Yes."

"So she offered you the silver of longing. Longing

and desire were a large part of your visit to Germany?"

"Yes."

"And she gave you the blue of the intellect and the blue of the heavenly. I wonder if it could have been this blue that wove your husband's dream? Perhaps it forced him to realize what he could never reach with you and he wrote you off as dead."

She thought for a time on this one before she nodded. "I guess you're right. It must have been something like that about me that turned him off. And I mean he really got turned off. And yet I'm not sure I was that unreachable."

"You were unreachable to him. What fires your imagination is precisely the things that we talk about and those that you read about endlessly. For these you are willing to devote your life or even gamble your life. How do I know this? Frankly, Madam, I have seen your dreams. And I have the sphinx. This animal goes back to the soul place and waits between the folds. It is a crouching and compound and ephemeral beast, for it is you and your seminal head and it is the beast and its seminal body. It supplicates until the dew of manna springs round about it. On this it thrives. Having answered the hard questions of the oak tree, it itself demands answers of all those who approach it.

"And then she vanished with your ring and you found her in a flat-roofed one room cube-shaped building that is a perfect simulacrum of the intellect. And in what position?"

"The lotus position."

"The position of highest intellectual endeavor where the soul is sought. Did it interest you that she denied taking your ring?"

"Yes, and it angered me too. Where else could it have gone? I think she was lying."

"If she had been lying would she have given you a ring of far more value than the first?"

"No. That doesn't make sense. Well, where did it go?"

"Perhaps the Dream Angels took it. You had no further need of it. You had matriculated through Germany and had burned up your longing. The blue and the beast had dream-destroyed your marriage. So they took it back and she gave you another ring. This one was truly exquisite. It was a finely chiseled gold snake with its tail in its mouth and one wing. Did you not graduate from the silver of longing to the gold of completion?"

"Why was she giving me rings? What do these mean?"

"The ring adorns and subtly binds the power of the hand. A true ring carries exactly your mark or sign and presents you into the world. Its signet sealed in wax is the proof image of you. The snake symbolizes all we have said and more, much more. Bent into a circle and biting its tail it becomes the symbol of eternity. Is not eternity the ultimate force that binds the fifth or life finger into constant submission and entrains the power of your hand?"

"Yes, I guess I see that. And the beautiful wing on the snake?"

"Listen! And I will tell you how dreams explain dreams. My great friend is a judge. He dreamed he was trying a case and the question before the bench was whether a certain creature could be adopted.

"'Well, why can't it be adopted?' he asked.

"'Because,' the lawyer who was arguing the case said, 'it is an Edge.'

"Not wanting to appear ignorant before the assembled court by admitting he did not know what an Edge was, he tried to gain information by artful questions, but finally had to ask. 'What is an Edge?'

"The lawyer said, 'an Edge is a navel with a feather in it,' and then the judge woke up.

"Can you see what this means?" Dr. Zvee looked at

her intently.

"I hate to disappoint you but I haven't the foggiest. Were you serious when you said this dream of the judge's explains my dream of the golden snake?"

"Why, yes," he said, "quite serious. Of course, you do have to know a bit of symbolic logic and then it fits quite well. Castaneda uses the word 'Edge' quite often. He describes its loss by the mother whenever she gives birth to the child, particularly the first-born. Having lost this Edge she can no longer be a warrior. The whole body, mind and soul expresses the will in the warrior. Small wonder this figure is so compelling. The navel focuses the beam of the will that it may be used in its naked power and the feather is the actual instrument by which flight is possible in birds. What he is saying is: a warrior with an Edge can fly with the will. Can you follow this?"

She had a rather grim look about her eyes like one whose concentration has failed her. "I think I follow some of it, but on the other hand, O.K., I'll admit the Edge flies on its will. But can we fly with only one wing?"

"Now you are catching on, Mrs. Darnely. Well reasoned. Yes. We may fly with only one wing. The will is the power of the flight and if we have enough power, as the rocket has power, we may fly indeed. Of course, once it is launched we have no further control over that flight. Think how carefully our scientists calculated the course to the moon! They were as the frog and the grasshopper who lose all control once they have jumped so they had to make the jump or the rocket take-off perfectly. Did you know the Romans wore a golden grasshopper or locust on their togas as a symbol of the courage of that insect? No? Imagine what it takes for the tiny grasshopper to commit to such a leap!" He watched the thoughts knitting themselves across her brows. "But we do not have to throw ourselves on the parabola of chance. We can intend and we can control our flight. We are able to guide the will. Do you know how we do that?"

"I believe you once mentioned the understanding in this context. Where is the understanding? In the back of the head, maybe?"

"Precisely! In the hind brain, and the will is usually thought of as originating in the heart. From there, it is projected forward through the umbilicus. If the will were a nozzle like a fire hose, would it not propel you backward as it erupted? Yes," he chuckled, "I think it would. So that is your will and your snake has great understanding if we may judge by your description of its wing size. You need but put the power to the power, Mrs. Darnely. You may both fly and control the good ship, *June.* Have you thought of the word, diploma?"

"No. I know it's what you get when you graduate from school."

"Certainly, and it means two wings. One can fly safely when one is thoroughly trained, when one has a good understanding."

"And that's what the wing on the snake means?"

"It's one meaning. Now I believe we have collated enough data that we may begin to understand the symbol of the serpent. It goes on its belly and its chest and it has neither arms nor legs, yet it flies swiftly across the land and sea. It is the personification of the guiding understanding flying on the wing of the power of the will."

"No wonder it understood all that was happening in the Garden of Eden! And all of that was in my dream and the judge's dream?"

"All of that."

"Did the judge understand it when you told him about it?"

"No. He has never heard of Castaneda and even when the dream was couched to him in symbolic terms, he found the interpretation rather 'fanciful' I believe, was the actual term he used."

"So, you took a dream of a man who had no idea

of its meaning and interpreted it through the words of another man who had certainly never heard of the dream and used it to interpret my dream which you knew nothing about until this moment." She exclaimed incredulously.

He stroked his chin and pushed his lips together. "Yes, I would say that was a fair description. Yes, that is what I did."

"But how could you? I mean, this is uncanny." She exclaimed.

His smile broadened into a laugh. "We have spoken of the language of symbolism, Mrs. Darnely. You know it exists. You also know it is universal and unchanging. Those who study and become proficient in it, like this Castaneda or his mentor, don Juan, will appropriately assign the apt meaning to the proper symbol. All we need do is follow their lead. Remember: Castaneda spent a vast amount of time in dreams, or in 'dreaming' as don Juan emphasized it. I am not at all surprised that his words are useful in this situation."

"Where else could you have gone to find meaning for these dreams?"

"There are three great languages, Sanskrit, Greek and Hebrew that have retained the ancient symbolic meanings. When you know how to consult these you can unravel dreams to some level. Also there are adepts even now: the yogis, the Zen masters, certain Sufis, and monks of all religions who have devoted time to this study. And always there are our poets and those who write the great story." He laughed again. "It is not as astonishing as it may seem. Not at all. But, we are not quite finished. You play out the final scene on the burning, empty sands. The woman reappears and together you confront the two golden serpents. What have you to say about this?"

She shook her head. "Aren't all sands created by the ocean?"

"Perhaps not all, but I suspect most are." He

watched her struggle with the thought.

"Well," her voice rose almost to a cry, "that must mean something!"

"Indeed it does. It means a great deal. For it is the moon that drags the sea to and fro across the junction of the water and the land. It is the moon that forms the beach, vacuuming and vacuuming that sand until only the pure silicate particles remain. The moon that waxes and wanes, building to the silver bright of full and diminishing to invisibility of the new. The moon, as ancient wisdom ascertained, that paradigms the intellect to struggle at the equilibrium where the self may be saved."

"Everything you say agrees with you. This dream is a dream of the intellect."

"Wisely spoken. And there are two serpents and again there are separations. Did you not have separations in your life at this time?"

"I did indeed. And why was I so sure the serpents wouldn't bite me?"

"Did not your finger bear a talisman of fortune? You had looked on the graven serpent of gold and the image of the golden serpent rendered the venom of the real vipers harmless to you. Do you not recall the Israelites in the desert? They were bitten by serpents and needed but to gaze upon the brazen serpent formed by Moses to recover from their venom."

She sucked her breath in deeply. "But I thought that serpent in the wilderness was only a magic, uh, trick . . ."

"It certainly was magic. On that we are quite agreed. Are you interested in this brazen serpent?"

"Yes, especially since I had this dream of the golden one."

"I have given it much thought. We do not know if there was some sympathetic magic in the brazen one that brought about the protection. Snake bites are still handled by using a tourniquet to control the flow of blood and venom. It is just possible that Moses found a way to reduce the blood supply to the bitten area by having his patients look on the brazen one. We do not know for sure. But, the principle is sound."

"Tell me about that."

"The principle is that the image of anything is as a door that gives a certain access to it. You probably know that primitive peoples refuse to have their picture taken, as they fear their souls will be stolen or the photographer will have gained power over them. That is the underlying logic of voodoo. As I said, this principle is correct even if it cannot be applied to all cases. Consider!" He leaned forward to better command her attention. "For millennia we did not know what caused infections. Then our scientists looked at bacteria. They gave us an image of them. All the experimenting we did but sharpened that image and gave us more insight into the life and needs of these little organisms. One day we found that nature had long ago devised ways of protecting fungi against these bacteria. When we added that fact to the image we already had built up, we gained a powerful control. Can you see how the image gives access to the object?"

She nodded slowly. "Yes, I believe I can see that. What Moses did was to set up the brazen serpent as an example of this principle. It apparently worked for the Israelites."

"Let us recapitulate this," he suggested. "First we assemble as complete a picture as possible of the object we wish to control. Then we use the facts in this image to do the actual controlling. In the intellectual world it is all done by making the mosaic of thought. In the physical it is all based on this thought mosaic and carried out by the hand, more specifically by the thumb and the forefinger touching in a circle. Precisely as the serpent of gold was curled into the circle of infinity. The thought mosaic is an image of carefully assembled and arranged ideas. Therefore, the idea is the operant tool and it is also the hone of the operant tool."

It was some time before she said, "that does make such good sense."

the ultimate reality
of dreams

June was in a square room with two women and a young man whom she could not describe, as he never stood directly in front of her. One woman was very large, bigger than the man, in a forest green dress that fitted loosely. She had big arms and a strong body. The other woman was the size of June. The square room was almost unfurnished. June did seem to see some things out of the corner of her eye but she could not really focus on them. There were no lights, no windows or doors.

She asked the man to help the big woman who was to be killed, for she was thinking strongly of her mother at that moment and was very concerned about her. But after thinking about it she hoped this death would not affect her mother. She again asked the man to help the big woman through her death, to cushion the blow when she was forced to realize that she was to be killed, to comfort and strengthen her that she might not be afraid. The man and the big woman left the room and she seemed to be left alone. She waited.

After awhile the man returned alone, and she knew the big woman was dead. Relief and even gladness soothed her now that it was done. The man seemed to be content with what had happened and he assured her that all went well. He waited for her to see something and finally she did. She could fully see what she had only glimpsed—a rectangular metal table with raised sides, like a hospital gurney. The small woman was lying on this table with a white sheet covering everything except her head. June wondered if the woman was also dead but, as she looked at her, the woman stirred and June knew she was alive. The woman moved more and June saw her eyes were open.

June thought, how wonderful! The big woman is dead but this woman is alive." She waited for someone to toss back the cover so the woman could rise and get off the table.

Her brother's call came in late afternoon. "June? I just called to tell you that mother died." She was not at all surprised. Myrtle was beyond her ninetieth year and had been slowly dying in the nursing home for a long time. "They took her to the hospital so she could die there. She just slipped away quietly. No pain, not even any discomfort that we could see. You coming home for the funeral?"

"No, I don't think so. You take care of the details. If you need anything let me know." She hung up slowly. Why go? Her brother had everything, the house, the farm and had pushed her out completely. She hardly needed another family fight. And, she loathed the idea of seeing the icy, rigid corpse that was the total, visible remains of her mother, the one person on earth with whom she was really close.

That night she dreamed of Myrtle but could not get close enough to talk to her. The following night it was the same, and the next night and the next for seven nights. After a solid week of trying, her desire to commune with this woman was so powerful and so intense that it permeated her entire day. Whatever differences lay between them—June's intense love of life and life of love that fear-wrapped the frigid heart of her mother: Myrtle's cold and forbidding posture that had shattered the will of her husband—they were still in those waters together and that would continue longer than June would believe. It is a truth that your daughter is your daughter all of your life and the further truth is that they loved each other. An even further truth of June and Myrtle was that they were bound together into eternity.

June went to sleep so quickly it was more of a capture than a process. She was immediately in a precipitous and geocentric flight that flung her into the base of the mountain and burst her into a small room. It was cut deep into the granite rock inside the great heart of the Blue Mountain Range. In front of her was a massive door of iron. A window about a foot square was cut through it at a comfortable level with her eye. A very large, dark haired and commanding woman was obviously in charge of the door. She stood aside and let June look through the window.

June saw beyond the door a long, curving passage-way with a very high ceiling that extended far beyond her vision into the granite rock. She could see all those who walked there but from their actions it was clear that they could not see her nor did they even know of the small room. For they came around the bend and moved straight toward her, often looking directly into her eyes. Then, with no hint of recognition they moved on past the door. Some were in pairs and some in groups and she knew they had died together. She saw Myrtle walking slowly along, alone and looking very sad, wearing the same old green coat and a rust colored velvet hat with its drooping pheasant feather that had protected her for so many of her life-years. She looked far younger than her death-time of ninety years, definitely younger even than the last time they had met on earth, and was carrying a purse June had given her.

The big woman motioned June back from the door, opened it and let Myrtle into the little room; then the woman stepped back. June looked intently into her mother's face and tried to talk with her. She spoke, called her by name, called her mother, friend, tried to touch her and begged her to talk. But Myrtle did not hear. She looked past her daughter with a blank stare at the far wall. June realized she had no breath. There was no movement of air or of her ribs.

"If she had died of some disease I could not catch it now because she has no breath," came into her mind as she continued her efforts at communication.

Suddenly, June was on a rocky beach. A half moon slung low in the sky, but it was a bright moon that gave a soft and reaching light to see by. She watched as her mother walked quickly toward her. Both were barefoot. Myrtle wore a deep blue, rather a cross between a sky and a midnight blue dress, with a four paneled skirt that June had never seen. They hugged each other, their forms were solid, and they could feel each to each. For the second time

June could feel as well as see in a dream. June's feelings of her mother hugging her were a lovely delight. They threw back their heads laughing, and happiness was the theme they reeled out and back and played over and over together. Joy and deep pleasure laced the words they exchanged with each other. But the scene shifted.

The big woman moved out of the shadows where she had been waiting, motioned June back from the door and ushered her mother out into the passageway. June watched the small green coat and lusterless hat as her mother, with a sad step, slowly disappeared among those who walked in death. Waking to the black of that night of intense loss and sadness June lay long, cradling her heart to rock away a bit of that lonely pain. But three weeks later it all reversed.

"We did it, Mom, we finally made it here."

"Yes, we did. We found the one place where we can talk and actually be together. June, we're together. This is the only place where we can do this. We can talk to each other and we can hug each other. Here we are solid just as we used to be. June, we are alive again and we are together. Here on this beach. Under the light of this moon and in the control of your far reaching love we are together."

All the pain was gone now in the triumph of their deed.

"Yes, in that mountain I could see you but you couldn't see me. But I could see you and I wanted to talk to you so badly. Oh, Mom, I wanted so much to talk and touch you."

"We've done it dear." And she threw back her head and laughed that full and good laugh that used to come at those moments when she and June were especially close. They sat on the rocks and listened to the sea and looked at each other. They laughed and they talked and finally said goodbye as they had done all their lives together. June turned to go because she had no choice. She hugged her mother again and felt the full, real feeling of flesh beneath her hands. Then she was compelled to end her visit.

"I'll be waiting for you," called Myrtle. As June took another step her mother's final words called clearly, slowly, and as distinctly as the tolling of slow bells, among the waxes of her mind, *"Yes, we will see each other again!"*

When June waked into the brightness of that day, she was full and happy. The dream was a sufficiency of delight. Not again did she need to meet Myrtle on the beach under the moonlight.

"How old were you then?"

"Fifty-four."

"And married to your second husband is spite of some good dream advice that you did not heed."

June looked at him ruefully. "Believe me, I would now. In fact, a year later I did listen to a dream and got rid of that . . ." she made a wry face and voice, ". . . man."

"Have you ever thought that marriage was invented to give us a foretaste of heaven and hell? Anyone who has lived through either a good marriage or a bad one clearly understands this. Well, what do you think? Was she real or not?"

June looked at the pleasure in his slightly smiling old face for he knew he had her in a bind; she wanted so desperately to believe. "This may sound slightly insane, but I think I really saw and felt my mother and I think I will see her again. Tell me the real truth."

"The real truth is what makes life such an exceptional cliff-hanger. We cannot know anything for a certainty and we cannot prove even that we exist. There's the rub, Mrs. Darnely, and there's the fun of it. We must proceed and act as though we were wise, knowing all the time that we think on sand." He laughed out loud and she was forced to join him for the ridiculousness of it all struck home.

"Then I didn't see my mother?" her voice was sad.

"On the contrary, I think you did."

"You do?" her voice crescendoed.

"For several reasons. First, you met her in the heart of the mountains in Sheol, hell, the underworld, call it as you will, and you did not succeed in talking to her or feeling her, nor did she recognize you. That scene could come right out of the Odyssey or any of the great books. Those in the rock, which is down, down in a sacred place, cannot be contacted. And, she wore green and brown, the colors of growth and earth. But up on the high beach she wore celestial blue and ran where the sand is and the moon rules and the tides run, there you not only talked to her as we are talking but you felt her. That is strong evidence of reality. You have only done that once before and you were probably dealing with a real creature at that time as well."

"You didn't tell me that."

"No, I was not anxious to encourage your belief in the reality of dragons. But mothers, well, frankly, I feel quite differently about mothers, especially your mother. I believe she is real and you are equally convinced. Thus, Madam, we may say that the evidence at hand encourages us to the belief that your mother is alive and waiting for you."

"Wow! That's fantastic!"

"Did you understand the color of the dress she wore?"

"Isn't blue the color of heaven and the intellect? I thought it was opposed to the red and black."

"I think that is as good an insight as you could have. Blue is all of that. But to continue. It is widely felt that the soul journeys for a time after death. That would explain your inability to meet her during the first week. Then, when you did meet, you saw her in a deep cave cut into the granite heart of the Blue Mountains. This is not unprecedented. Ulysses and other classical heroes have gone down to visit the dead with equally unsatisfying results. What is unprecedented is your meeting on that beach. We have talked of beaches before but I do not believe we have defined them. Would you like to give us a definition of beaches?"

She finally shrugged her shoulders. "A beach is where the land and the water meet." Her face bore a rather helpless expression.

"Excellent, Mrs. Darnely, excellent. That's where time is born. The land was called 'Earth' by God and therefore represents the earthy parts of us. To reach it in your dream you had to rely on your left hemisphere—the proof is that the moon furnished the total illumination. But your mother had to traverse the great waters to reach that beach and she came by sea. 'One if by land and two if by sea,'" and the delight of his contagious smile flowed onto her face.

"So that's it. I had to come by my intellect; she had to come by her soul. But of course. Of course. Of course. She's dead. And for our meeting we chose—"

"If you will permit me, I believe it was you who chose. It was the power of your love that brought her up to that beach and under the thrall of a rational moon."

"I chose the beach where we could come by land or water and meet under that bright moon?"

"Yes. The same moon that turns off that little inhibitory gland that hangs in the middle of your head. And when it does it releases all the energy of your pituitary to drive the decision of your meeting ground."

"That's neat. Will I see her again?"

"She has promised you will. I have no doubt she will keep her promise. But we have not adequately discussed the dream in the small square room and I feel it deserves better. We could easily pass this off as a prognostic dream and wonder at our Dream Angels' prescience. I believe this would not do justice to this dream. Certainly, it did prepare you for your brother's phone call, but it indicates far more. The big woman in the green dress, again that green intrudes itself, is your mother, but in a specific sense. Myrtle was actually a small woman. But she was large in your eyes as a guide and a source of moral reasoning. You had not followed her desires for you and had run into the world and lived it, as she was prone to say, 'to the hilt.' You know how she disapproved of that. Now you have rid yourself of those illusions and you no longer need her in that role. She is led off to die. My, my, how carefully that dream was prepared for you. For when she died both her governing role was removed and, most importantly, the strong drives and passions that strove in her and burgeoned in you died. Her death changed you and brought you low but it did not kill you. You were protected by the metal table under you. It was one such as hospitals use. You had undergone a lessening like a surgical removal and were recovering under that white sheet. The new June Darnely was about to step forward and death could not reach you there. You would step into the room with no doors and no windows. In that upper room which is highly suggestive of the room in your head you observed the series of actions that described the freeing of June from Myrtle. I believe you like that room for you surely have been there quite often."

"Did I save the best of my mother? Did I throw away any that I should have kept?"

"It would seem to me that you did it quite correctly and have retained only as much baggage from that auspicious lady as is good and proper for this life. But, please remember that teachers are not without their prejudices even as their students are not." They laughed together.

"A little poem occurs to me. Would you like to hear it?"

"Oh, yes."

He leaned back and in his deep and rough voice chanted:

certitude

They met on the night of a moon-bright shore
On a beach where the sarsens play,
One had escaped from a dungeon of stone
And one from the light of the day,
And their joy was a spark of a lightning of arc
That bound them together alway.

"Is that your poem, Dr. Zvee?"

"I am never sure. I think it is mine but it could be one I learned so long ago I have even forgotten the task of memorizing it."

June Darnely floated back to her home that evening.

corollary dreams of equal reality as related by Ivan, age forty-four

"I had gone to bed late that night or early in the morning if you prefer. The moment I fell asleep, I was laying on a beach on my left side facing the water and eating fish. Not more than three meters from me another figure, exactly my size, but clothed in a gleaming white seamless gown that covered him completely, was lying on his right side and also facing the sea. We were lying head to head. I tried to communicate with this person. The sun was shining with an even light and I knew it was day. My efforts with the fish grew more frantic as I tried to tell this being that I was desperately in need of food. I had my head thrown far back to look at him but he continued to fiddle with his fish. Suddenly he looked up and I was looking into a face that was exactly and precisely my own. The shock of this was immense and climaxed my intense agitation. I was twenty-six.

"At thirty-three I had a sudden vision while I was trying to take a nap. I had not fallen asleep but I saw the face of an old man, serene and calm in a field of lilies. Four days later I had a similar vision but this time I saw a young man in the lily field. He looked very much like the older man. It was perhaps six weeks later that I met with a group of friends who were going to a lecture. I didn't want to hear it but afterwards they suggested that I meet the woman who gave it. She and I talked at some length and she went to her car to get me a book she thought I would like to read. When she handed it to me I was most deeply troubled for the dust jacket contained exactly the image of the young man on the front and the old man on the back. She told me that they were Sufis and that the young man lived in Paris. In the book was a picture of his house but no address. I went to Paris soon after and walked the streets praying until I found at last the house and met him. He told me he was not my master but his father, who had been dead for many years, was. His father was the one responsible for my visions. He then led me through the steps of the Sufi initiation. I passed them quickly and began giving services in the church. In a short time I was made head of all the Sufis in Norway.

"On May 29, 1994, after we talked late into the night, I dreamed that the room was full of people. Two women stood out from the rest, embracing each other in a frankly lesbian fashion but fully clothed and well behaved.

A large man with a heavy body appeared. He had an unearthly appearance with three grooves on each side of his forehead that ended on top of his skull. His third eye was bright and shone with a more brilliant life than his lateral eyes and he focused all of the elements of the dream in himself.

"He said: 'It is hard to understand when you are here as you can see only a part. It is the whole that is important.' His face was like mottled marble, flesh-colored and green. He continued: 'People work against each other.'

"I awoke at this point and saw a partly transparent figure about human size beyond the end of my bed. It had light or energy lines that ran vertically down it and was back-lit with an egg shape of illumination. I saw this figure in three-quarter view that ended at the waist; it had no legs. It moved slowly across the end of the bed. It did not speak but I understood it very clearly.

"It said: 'I am here and I want you to know I am here. I will be back.' I felt no fear and this surprised me very much. Of course I had had no experience with this type of visitation before, but I continued to be surprised that the interview was very peaceful and very quiet and very powerful."

"And how does this make you feel?" Dr. Zvee asked.

"Frankly, I feel I'm more of a warrior and I'm happier with myself since we met."

"Even meeting such visions as your leg-less phantom?"

"As I said, I really wasn't that bothered by it. I knew it was somehow connected with you and that may have been what took the fear away. But," he shrugged, "maybe such visions are fearful only if the phantom wishes it to be so. Do you know why it had no legs?"

"They never do. Legs are a condition of this world only. Once you leave here you neither need nor have them.

Besides, it is written that God hates the horse and the legs of a man. Are we agreed then that all of these dreams you have just recounted are reality and true experiences?" Dr. Zvee asked.

"Quite agreed."

"Then it was yourself you saw on that beach?"

"Yes."

"It is widely rumored that meeting oneself in dreams is deadly. And now we know that it is not nearly as deadly as these rumors suggest. You saw yourself and you are preserved. There are several points that are most instructive about that experience. First, it occurred when you were twenty-six, the age of calcification, when the spine is at its full strength and the energies are at their maximum. That was the only time you could have mar-shaled enough energy and had the enduring strength to meet that self. Second, you were lying head to head as though you were hinged. You can see if the hinge were closed you would be face to face. Is it not probable that you saw the very mirror image in which you were created? For it had a seamless garment that covered it to the ground."

"I think it had to be, for it was myself, exactly myself in every way!"

"I enjoy this little game so indulge me. Would this figure have its heart on the right or left side?"

"I've thought of that before. He would have his heart on the right."

Dr. Zvee laughed deeply. "You are so right, my friend, so right. The two afternoon visions of the older and younger man. It is quite certain they are not dreams."

"Quite certain. They were planned to get me to Paris and they did a good job."

"And you just went by yourself with no idea where to go or what to do and you found the younger man? How long did it take you?"

"Two days."

"Good heavens. It is obvious that you were guided and very strongly. The third dream is amazingly interesting. The two women caressing set the stage for a nonproductive event. I am sure you understand that. And the man. You say he had six grooves in his forehead that ran into his hair line?"

"Yes, six, and a third eye."

"I have seen one man with such grooves in his forehead. I do not know what it means to be so marked. Time will unveil this, I am sure. Do you know the meaning of that third eye?"

"Certainly. It is the pineal gland and it is on fire and that is where he is seeing and acting. He set the stage for the phantom to appear."

"Yes, quite so. The two are one in many ways. When one appears the other cannot be far behind. Well, Ivan, you have had a most interesting excursion into the burden of the spirit. It will be of the greatest interest to see where it will all lead. There are very profound changes coming to fruition in the near future. Changes that have already cast their shadows before them. All you have seen will have remarkable relevance."

chapter eleven

the joker and the jokee

Her second husband and she were seated in the large gymnasium at her high school, converted for the occasion with rows of hard wooden folding chairs. A play was in progress and a number of students in ordinary clothes were moving woodenly and mumblingly through their roles on the battered old stage. Except for one. This character was quite aware, moved smoothly and June concluded it must be a devil, as it seemed to have no head. To and fro on the stage and then the headless creature moved down among the viewers and walked back and forth in front of them. No other person seemed to notice.

She excused herself, went out the back door into the schoolyard and walked rapidly along a bumpy dirt road. It was dark but she could see clearly. She came to a forest where she left the dirt road and moved onto soft and lush green grass. The light of twilight glowed in the sky now and she could see even better. She sensed more than heard someone or something following her. She turned to look. A quick panic hit her. A lion was walking at her pace, eyes looking at the ground, about twelve feet behind her. She continued to walk fearfully. But when she looked back again, her Persian cat Sinhue was walking beside him and she realized she was safe from that danger; unfortunately she was deep into the woods and totally lost.

"The twilight will soon turn to night and I would be a lot better off out of this forest. I wonder if the forest animals have a path anywhere that I could follow out?" she asked grimly under her breath.

She looked up and saw a beautiful deer with magnificent antlers running on a wide grassy path. She followed as fast as her feet would take her but he was quickly out of view. Acute loneliness for the lovely animal oppressed her as she walked on, finally coming to a large pond or small lake in the midst of a lush green area surrounded by beautiful trees.

As she looked at the water, a new and strange voice seemed to come from over her left shoulder. She heard: "The outcome of this adventure depends entirely on you. Your life is at stake. In the water is a crocodile and you must go in the water and fight him. If you do not do this you will die here. If you do not do this you will die here. If you do not do this you will die here."

"This is ridiculous!" She turned around but could find no source for the voice. "I have no business fighting crocodiles or anything else at my age. I'm fifty-five years old and am certainly beyond that sort of thing."

"Your age or your sex are of no consequence. I

have told you what you must do. Do it!"

Having no choice, she jumped in the water and the crocodile came to meet her. They wrestled and rolled over and over and churned up the water into a thin mud soup. She felt no pain nor any real fear nor could she feel even the skin of the crocodile. Then a great laughter filled the forest, echoing and re-echoing among the tall trees. Her head came up abruptly and she saw the crocodile standing on his tail like a man, half of its body out of the water. His head was thrown back and it was obviously he that was making such a noise.

She got slowly out of the water and said to herself. "Well, this was all a joke!" Then she realized the night had passed and the light of day brightened up the dense green walls of trees. Still laughing, the crocodile slowly swam away.

She was pondering on getting out of the woods when she saw a large white house to her left. She flew quickly up to the third or fourth floor. She was sure she was on the third or fourth floor because, as she stood in the middle of this room, she could see the tree tops through the floor-to-ceiling windows in front of her. This was a large room consistent with the size of the house, possibly sixty or more feet square, beautifully furnished with chairs, tables, sofas, artwork, and multi-colored carpets—a great wide, bright and airy room without a single door. She was wondering how one gets out of such a door-less room when she noticed a man standing to one side of the tall windows.

He wore a multicolored robe of deep red, blue and green trimmed in silver and gold. It fitted loosely and reached to the floor. His head was even more riveting than his robe for it was perfectly round, perfectly bald and his face was friendly and genial and emitted a very gentle light. For all this, he really did not appear strange to her.

She asked him, "how do I get out of here?" He

threw his arms up toward the windows in front of her and they flew open.

He said in a loud voice of command. "Fly!"

She stepped up on the edge of the window and looked down on a beautiful green park-like lawn touched up with some ancient and spreading trees. A carpet appeared at her feet. The cords on both ends were raised up like handles. She stepped onto the carpet, took a firm grip of the handles and flew off, watching the deep green forest pass beneath her.

"My, oh my, oh my. Sometimes dreams drown us in a plethora of signs and meanings and this one over-exuberates with beauty. It would be so simple if we just knew where to begin. You asked what Type-3 dreams do, and I did not give you a truly complete answer at that time. What did you do after this dream?" Dr. Zvee asked.

"At that time? What did I do? I divorced him. The very next day I filed for my divorce. Within a month, I was rid of my second husband. And I decided never to even consider marriage again and most certainly to avoid that illusion like a deadly plague. Yuch! I definitely did not, do not, need that! Yes, I see now. I see very clearly at least something of what dreams do. This dream showed me how absolutely and completely ludicrous sex is and how shallow as a basis for any type of lasting relationship."

"Did you figure that out because of the crocodile?"

"I suppose he was part of it. Is he a critical actor here?"

"Quite critical. He stands at the head of the monsters of illusion. As you probably know, the crocodile is active only when the sun heat energizes his torpid body. The sun is compared to certain embellishments of the male body, which must be active in the mechanics of courtship and marriage. Also, the crocodile is unique among animals in that it eats people and can break the strong legs of a virile man with a quick sweep of its tail. It is wise not to stand too close to a mature crocodile for it will torpedo you. A further clue to the crocodile's nature was the extremely lush and verdant greenery about the lake." He chuckled. "An excess of fertilization is giving us rather over-much of that symbol. As we mentioned, this dream does tend to belabor us with its symbolism. You might say it brags like a particular pregnancy we are most anxious to hide."

"Was I in some danger?"

"Not in this dream as only your sight was involved. And dreams do have their safety features much as automobiles have airbags. But let us review this dream. You and your second husband are watching a play performed by untrained young people. All theater is a simulacrum of life, we watch ourselves as we go through our lives and we see both sides. We see ourselves as actors and as audience, but that acted by ingenuous youth is particularly close to life. Their very lack of finesse magnifies the vitality of the work they do. And this little charade on or off the stage consumes our attention and we call it reality until the devil appears without a head, a creature of all flesh, and walks to and fro and up and down before us to show us that what we thought was real is certainly not real. Then are we forced to go out of our backs, to leave by the rear door and tread a rough path to the forest.

"This is the place of irrational creatures, very similar to a garden. And there, twelve feet behind you, was a lion that walked harmoniously with your cat, creatures of the night whose eyes shine so they can go into the thick darkness. Lions have a great roar and they crouch down to become sphinxes. And we find the deer there whose antlers have grown under the driving male power into the air of heaven like symmetrical and stable roots. Will he be nourished on high if his herbage here fails? Is there manna for the deer? We humans may grow roots into rivers but they are not so elegantly obvious. Whichever type you follow, your task is to wrestle the crocodile and then you may follow the path of your will. On the first level he is that primal urge and you wrestled with him and found it was all a joke. But he is more than that—the crocodile lacks a pineal gland and attacks and eats man. Having put the crocodile in his place, you may then fly to the upper room.

"And this pool or lake. It is as I have dreamed before?" June asked.

"Ah, yes, for there are many things that grow and tantalize in such a water. In this dream it was a crocodile but in others you may find many far more interesting objects."

"Why did I fly to the third or fourth floor?"

"That was very cleverly worked out by your dream. For the third floor is the top of the physical, and the fourth is the floor of the intellect. Your dream gave you both. This room is very well described in *Der Golem* as a room that has only one entrance or exit and that approach is below ground. This is also the upper room in which Christ ate with his apostles. But your dream does it even better, for only windows, the eyes of the soul, look out onto the trees and lawn. To get to this room where you are totally withdrawn into your head, you must have the courage of flight.

"When you become more conversant with the moon you will not wonder that the man had a round, bald head and suffused a gentle light in the room. The colors of his robe are those of the light spectrum. The man may be said to be clothed in copper, for copper exists in three primary colors, red as the metal, blue as the solution, and green as the oxide, and he wears the coat of Joseph, of many colors reaching to the ground. The silver of longing and the gold of intellect stitch him together. And the copper gives him his ability to open those great windows, for that is what hardens and browns him, and gives him that great strength."

"I thought the primary colors were red, yellow and blue."

"Indeed, the pigment spectrum is based on red, *yellow* and blue, but the light spectrum is based on red, *green* and blue. Of course, his robe reaches the floor for the moon is totally clothed in her light and if she, oops! I do think we should say he, and if he is not clothed in light we cannot see him."

"Is the moon male or female?"

"It depends on whom you ask. I always think of it as female as it waxes and wanes and controls the menstrual cycle, while the sun burns continually like the male pituitary under the lash of its stimulating hormones. But many, many cultures refer to it as male. In German it is *Herr Mond and Frau Sonne,* Sir Moon and Mrs. Sun. Primitive cultures frequently call the moon the fertilizer of the woman and think of it as male. It may seem a bit ludicrous to us to blame the moon for an unwanted child, but it was actually looked on as the agent that did the deed. The male partner in this case is thought to only be acting as an opener of the vaginal channel. You may have your choice, Mrs. Darnely, for there is tremendous weight, thought, history and precedent on each side."

"And the flying carpet?" June asked.

"Just like Sinbad; I would wager you were an excellent pilot. The carpet is made just so big and of just certain materials and woven in a certain way. It is the carpet of temperance that flies you out of the prison of your own head. And that is exactly the counsel you need to get out of the upper room. This temperance, everything in moderation, nothing in excess, is the clutch of ideas that leads us into the world and is the balance point on which success in life depends. Briefly we may note that what you lost when you divorced was gained back in the power to levitate that carpet. It is said that the sum total of energy and matter and their interchange remains constant in the universe."

She smiled. "So I lost a husband and gained a carpet."

"I would say, Mrs. Darnely, that you were richly over-paid."

"I agree with you completely, Dr. Zvee. Not only did I gain a carpet but I cleared out a lot of closet space for my own things. It's win-win as I see it." And they both laughed. Later, she often wished she had asked him who he thought the joker and the jokee really were.

chapter twelve

seeking the teacher and the way out

S he had returned to the university and was walking among the administration buildings late in the evening. She recognized the buildings but the one she actually went into was not at all familiar. Inside was a large hushed room filled with tables where students were bent over their books. She wanted to leave and saw a door that looked like it led to the outside but in some way she knew this door was forbidden to all ordinary persons. A well-dressed woman approached and told her that she could go through the door and opened it for her. Outside, she walked a few steps and stumbled over a young man and woman who were lying on the ground in a very close position. Her new, black purse fell from her hand. Immediately, the woman got up to help her find it. While June was feeling on the ground for it, her hand hit a paper object. She picked it up and looked at it carefully. She could see it was folded into four parts and there was enough moonlight to reveal it as a $20 bill. She held this treasure tightly in her hand. The woman said she had found June's purse and handed it to her. But what she got was very old and worn, and made of green animal skin. Thanking the couple she walked away and shrugged her shoulders about the loss of the new purse. The $20 bill was consolation enough.

The scene changed abruptly—she was riding on top of some vehicle that was going through a very long black tunnel. There could have been other people inside the vehicle but she was alone on top. She thought that the tunnel would never end. Idly, she began to look at herself and was surprised to realize that she was not properly dressed. She had no bra and was wearing a T-shirt. In her right hand was a man's shirt that was dirty and smelly with sweat. She looked at it and smelled the rank odor with revulsion. But when she looked again she saw that her hand was really holding a nice clean blouse instead of the dirty shirt and she carefully put it on. Now fully dressed, she shot abruptly out of that tunnel and into a bright, very bright, lighted area that shone like a new city but was rather more like a circus.

She walked between the rides and the barkers, the lights and the noise, and thought, "there is no one here who knows anything. I can't talk to these people." But her hand slipped into the square pocket of her blouse and felt the great comfort of the $20 bill. "It's all right. I can make a phone call." She saw a phone booth, entered and closed the door before she realized she could not use a $20 bill in a pay phone.

She awoke and looked at the clock. "Its 2:30 am on April 7 and not another soul in this house." For a few moments the peace of being alone caressed her, then she began to think of her life and where it seemed to be going. "Maybe April is the cruelest month. Here I am sixty-two. I'm still trying to cope and learn something about my life but I seem to be going more blindly with every passing day. And there are very few of these days left. I must make that phone call." Her heart shuddered at the thought of him possibly refusing. "But at least I'll know. If he lets me come . . . ," she would not let even her mind frame the word "salvation" however appropriate it might seem, " . . . then my problems are solved. If not, I won't be any worse off." She shrugged mightily. By mid-morning her resolve had reached its sticking pitch. She dialed the operator and asked for time and charges.

It was answered by a deep, even gruff, old voice. "Hello?"

"Dr. Zvee? This is June Darnely. I am having some problems, I guess you could say."

"I hope they are not serious. Is your health all right?" The voice softened in concern.

"Oh, yes, I'm quite healthy. It's not that. It's, well, frankly, I think I have to have someone help me to understand and you're the only one I know of anywhere. This is a terrible imposition, I know that, but would it be possible for me to visit you? I mean," she added hastily, "I won't be any bother to you. I hate to ask to take up your time like this, but I'm convinced you are the only one who could understand and help."

"That is very flattering, Mrs. Darnely. If I can be of

help, I should be delighted to do so. If you wish to visit me please come. How soon could you get here?"

"I can take a train and be there by tomorrow afternoon. Would that be all right? I mean, is that all right?"

"Yes, certainly. I will expect you tomorrow. You know where my house is? Very good. Good-bye." The operator came back on the line and told her the call was $20.00.

She caught the train at noon and that night as she fell asleep in her reclining seat to the steady click-clack of the steel wheels on the steel track, she slipped into a life boat sitting on the right side of the stern and looked intently at the eight or ten other persons seated in front of her. They were staring forward so she never saw their faces but from the way they sat and scanned the horizon she knew they were trapped and rather desperately seeking some way out. She looked around. They were in the middle of a large perfectly circular pond, ringed on every side with thick jungle of a deep, rich green. The leaves were large and she could see details of some of them from her boat. The unbroken wall of forest in front of her was a solid pale of steel bars; the intense fear of entrapment on that tiny pond vibrated between her and her shipmates.

"But there is an inlet behind us," she thought, "that leads to the sea. Then we are free." She turned and there behind her was exactly that inlet and exactly that sea. And she could see the far horizon. She woke with a great sigh of relief and went to breakfast.

As she walked up the long walk to the front door, the big man with the white beard that stood a head taller than others about him, opened it and stood laser-straight, awaiting her approach. The afternoon sun cast a halo about his balding head and wispy hairs, and the broad, and handsome old face that still looked pink and young was set in the grip of his iron control. For a moment it fleeted across her mind: "I know now what Jacob meant when he looked at Esau, 'looking on you is like looking on the face of God.'"

He extended his hand as he said. "Good afternoon, Mrs. Darnely. I have been expecting you. I believe we have a great deal to discuss."

"And how are you, Dr. Zvee?"

"Better, Mrs. Darnely, better now that you are here. Do come in." He turned her past him into the clean, white room, seated her on the soft, comfortable couch, and himself on a rigid, straight-back chair. After a few random questions he said, "so, you have come to discuss your dreams."

She thought for long, long moments. "I guess, I really have come just for that. Yes, they told me to stop wandering, to come where I can get order in my thought; to bring these problems to you." She indicated a thick sheaf of typed pages. "As you see, I've had many of them. Since I was eight years old."

"Would you like to start with the one that brought you here?"

"Yes, I would. And I had one on the train that I would like your comments on as well."

"Have you specific questions about these two dreams?"

"No, I would just like to hear whatever you say. You know my needs far better than I do." She sat tensely forward on her soft couch and watched his face and his strong hands that held his chair in a vice grip.

"Your courses at the university and the life you have there are darkened by the realization that they are not completely meaningful. You are interested in even more than the didactic life. This interest and the power of the Angels of Dreams combine, and when they join to drive to the goal, you are driven indeed. This is Dream Persistence which has all the stubborn inexorability of overwhelming fate and it wanted you to find a teacher so it showed you the exact path you should follow. You had to enter new and unfamiliar territory on both the mental and physical levels. The building, filled with students busily reading, was as much an indication of the necessity of accepting new ideas as the necessity of welcoming new surroundings. The busy students are the sign of the way you must work: you are to be a student of the book.

"And this path, since it goes beyond even the didactic, is for you alone. Therefore, you go through a certain door that is barred to everyone else and your guide for this is a certain elegant lady that looked quite a bit like yourself. The door was critical in another way as no other exit would have put you in contact with the couple. Their position and the way you tripped over them clearly showed you had lost interest in that type of thing as did the fact that you lost your black purse. The black purse is the symbol of most intense heat. Our scientists know this as the most intense radiator of energy and call it black body radiation. But this couple did find a purse for you, an old green one. It does look as if you yet will be creative. And then you found your moon gift, that all important $20.00 with its fours. Did you notice the bill was folded into four parts? The pocket had four sides. May I ask how much the long distance call cost?"

"Twenty dollars."

"How perfectly do dreams sum their effects, and it even told you what to do when it took you into that phone booth. It may have all been a dream but this money gave you the courage to call. There are other interesting uses for twenty—fingers and toes, the months in the Mayan year— and these further give you the power to move. Then, you went through a tunnel that seemed endless and very dark; the almost impossible transition from the institution of learning that is driven by the pure intellect to the whirling circus world. This long, black journey is the tunnel of desire that leads from the intellect of the university to the circus of the world. This circus of turning wheels and loud noises is founded on desire and feeds upon it and pulls the First Illusion over its head. It revels in the rage of reproduction. On these wheels turn all the life that floats on this earth.

"In the tunnel you found to your surprise that you were not properly clothed and were holding a man's stinking, sweaty shirt. You rapidly substituted a clean blouse and that puts men just about where they belong." He laughed with her.

"It did serve to reaffirm your vow concerning matrimonial attachments, particularly after the chilling realization that you were trapped in a circus world of tinsel and bounce with no one to talk to. You were not satisfied with the university and you were turned off by the circus world. How vitally, vitally important it is to have even one person to share your thoughts when your predicament seems so insoluble."

"It does sort of give away my true feelings, but I really don't think all men are that bad." They laughed some more. "The circus world is what I thought it was then?"

"Yes, exactly and your dream left you trapped there. You realized this was the throbbing doom of perdition for you and you had to find a way out. You were given not only the $20.00 but also that perfect little dream on the train. Shall we look at that now?" She nodded.

"The small boat is your head. Remember that a small boat has a different meaning from a large one. The small boat is a dream device to put you into the four dimensions and give you mental stability just as a small, real boat gives you physical stability on an unstable medium. You orient yourself to the boat and that orients you in your head. The difficult acts are to orient the boat on its water, which requires the compass, and to unlock the orientation of your mind from the boat or from your head, which the boat represents.

"Your companions were sitting forward in the boat and they were locked into it. Their forebrains were caught into the four dimensions of this world and they could not escape. Of course, they could not escape—they could not even look around because they did not know how to turn. They did not even know that such an act as turning was possible. But you did. Neatly done, Mrs. Darnely, neatly done!" He smiled widely. "If Sartre had known of your dream he would never had written *No Exit*. He would have realized exactly what you have made so clear tonight; there is an exit, and it is exactly behind us. Just as Castaneda found out when he developed the second face of the warrior. Why do we affix the seal of greatness to these ancient prophets and Biblical figures? Because they gave us an exit. And you were sitting in the back of the boat. You were in your hind brain or right brain and in that position you were able to turn, and turning you found your way out." His voice had become almost loud. Now he was silent for a moment in his admiration of her dream actions.

"So this dream is meaningful?" she asked.

"Extremely, Mrs. Darnely, extremely. Something or someone up there is jerking our chains, as the young people say. Every time I am driven into a problem and cannot find the path of solution that leads out of it, a dream seems to come to untie its knot. Now you can readily see; perhaps the most important reason for sending the Type-3 dreams is—*to show us the way out.* Can you follow that?" His voice rose in the excitement of confirming fact to fact.

"I think I can. In fact, all my dreams have been telling me the same thing. When I was in the water, the Serpent of Separation offered me the chance and the path to freedom, at least from my family. Then my Woman of Light was ready to lead me across and free me completely from this world if I wanted to go. Every other of my Type-3 dreams has carried the same message. I can get out anytime

I want and I *don't* have to die to do it."

"Beautifully said, Mrs. Darnely, beautifully said. Dream-turning whipped you back to the vast sea where the Second Illusion can be perforated by the rashly brave. From the four dimensions to the wide and infinite sea, and all that was required of you was to turn in your head. To turn *in* your head, as one does in dreams, rather than to *turn* your head as one does while awake. That gave you a way out. I am sure you noticed that none of your dream colleagues thought to look around to find that escape channel so clearly present behind you. This is because you have control over this little boat and have to do the proper thing to get out of that cove. You did, indeed, do the proper thing. We will see other examples of this turning as we go through other dreams."

"What does the train mean?"

"Different conveyances tend to symbolize different things. A train exemplifies the thrust of pure will to the goal. You know of course that the engineer is driving it but you never think about him. No one ever seems to be driving a train. Have you not noticed that it seems to move by itself?"

"Yes, I have noticed that. It's so impersonal."

"On this train you were alone, roaring down the directing rails that guarantee you will reach the goal. And of course, here you are."

They smiled comfortably together before he continued. "You have conquered the First Illusion and now there is only one mode of excitement left; the Second Illusion and the possibility of entrance into all the beauty that art and music and drama have siphoned out of eternity. You continue to need the guide that will put meaning into your life by bringing you face to face with this cold illusion and its reality.

"And that is what dreams do. They position us to assess our life and give it substance by our loves and by our death. These great dreams play upon their stages all that meaning, meting it out spoonful by spoonful, until we have engulfed life's pallid lump and flamed upon our palates in the crimson heats of youth, and the azure isolation of old age. What then *is* this life of ours? Is it not a transience, pale and yellow, that folds its shoulders down and bears between them?"

a corollary dream that finds a way out: Tad, age thirty-two

It was low tide for him. Divorced, out of college, no job, he was standing on the sand about twelve feet from the roll of the tide. The moon lighted the scene. To his left a large black man stood, said nothing, but communicated with him in great clarity. He said a tidal wave of massive destructive power was coming and many would die, but for Tad there was a way out. Tad looked before him and there was a ladder reaching high into the heavens. He thought how he would climb it and wondered how soon the wave would reach him.

"So, Mr. Darnely, did you think the black man's name might be Cinderella?"

"No, no I didn't. How could you call him that? I thought Cinderella was a young girl."

"You are exactly correct but Cinderella means the soul burned to a cinder and that would explain why your soul is black. I know an artist who portrays the infinite—or even God as she says—as black men whose soul is burned to a cinder. And his mode of communication?"

"He didn't need to say anything. I knew exactly what he was talking about and what I needed to learn from him."

"He stood to your left between the ocean and the land; between non-being and being. As you know, this is the side of your spirit and soul. You may also look upon him as your id and certainly as the companion that communicates through your right hemisphere. This is the time of the dark brother, your brother. How fortunate you are. Your early warning system is watching out for you. Many will die but you, my friend, will live. You have been given a ladder and it is your way out. I know you thought long on the vision of Jacob in Haran. He called the place Bethel, House of God. It is said that this ladder is ascended and descended by Angels of God but it is also ascended by prophets. Mark that! The journey starts from the earth. Perhaps you are to be a prophet or an angel. We shall see. Do you know what disaster he is referring to?"

Tad replied, "it didn't come off. Very little talk about it now. Sounds like Nostradamus forecast it back in the fifteen hundreds. I guess there's someone already in the world, born February 4, 1962, that's about ready to come out and do something. Do you know what he'll do?"

"There are many abominations in this life-world of ours. I can imagine a vast clearing away of debris."

"What should we do?"

"Siddhartha put it so well: 'I can think, I can wait, I can fast. And, oh yes, I can compose poetry.' Three things we also can do, and a fourth, if our pain heightens to a certain intensity. Is that enough for you?"

"I believe that's just about the whole ball of wax."

the way out and where it may lead

When she was sixty-eight Mrs. Darnely had this disturbing dream.

"I am driving my now owned car on a highway, going to a certain city, and I believe Tad is in the car with me. He is a young boy of eight or ten. It turns out to be a very long drive and the only time I speak to him is to say this highway is the long way: I ought to have taken another shorter route. After what seems to be two hundred or more miles, we enter a metropolitan city of great size and population. Cars and people are everywhere. I drive for miles looking for an exit. I stop and ask people how to get to the highway home but these people will not answer. I park the car and go inside a public place to inquire. It turns out to be a tremendous mall with people everywhere. The place is huge and filled with shops. We cannot find a way out. No one is helpful and everyone is going about in a great hurry.

"We wander in and out of shops and through an open door that takes us into a private apartment. A man and wife are taking a nap. He remains on the bed covered but she gets up and is wearing white undergarments. She is quite pretty. She is friendly and appears to be communicating something to me, sort of waving her arms and pointing but I cannot understand a word. We leave.

We continue looking. I realize the car is parked far away and I don't know how to get back to it. The mall is on several levels. Tad looks down on a lower level and suddenly says, "I see it." He runs down the stairs and makes a right turn, then a left and as he turns the corner, I see just the top of his head, which now does not look like Tad's head.

I know he finds the exit but he does not come

back. I walk down the stairs to that level and look for him, but some time passes and I feel he will not return. He has either gotten lost or has been abducted. I walk back up the stairs. There seem to be thousands of people in this place, all moving rapidly here and there. I'm feeling rather dismayed and worried about Tad. I'm standing on the stairs near the top.

Suddenly a group of women surround me, excited and talking. I can understand them fine. They say there is a sign on me or a name; they press closely around and peer at my forehead. They all want one of these signs or names and wonder where I got it. I tell them I don't know what they see. I look down at my clothes, at my dark blue suit and can see nothing unusual. I tell them I only want someone to help me find my son. They don't want to leave but finally tell me there is another woman whom they will call. They do this and leave.

The other woman comes close to me. She is very friendly and looks a little like the woman who was taking a nap but now she is dressed. She has the same dark hair but is more mature. She says she hates to give me bad news but the police are searching all the theaters in the city, as there has been a rash of young boys kidnapped. I know my son or the boy I thought was my son cannot return. I tell the woman that I have been waiting there a long while and look at my watch. It reads exactly seven o'clock and I wake.

"Such a sad dream that plays upon the universal separation theme—the son must leave; the mother must grieve. But such a complex path to the next generation, and grandchildren are delightful," said Dr. Zvee.

174

the last meeting

June was in a room full of people where a large party was going on. She moved out of this into the hall and found Tibor there. He was lying on a couch but she really saw only his head. He seemed to be asleep or entranced or maybe just drunk.

She said, "I will kiss you." He turned his cheek to her and she said, "No! On the mouth!" She kissed him.

A man at her left shoulder whom she never really looked at said, "I know you're working on a picture. We'll get a lot of money for it." She turned away from Tibor and asked the man to take her to her room. Instantly she was outside the building and the man was gone. She walked along slowly.

About sixty feet away to her left was a block of four white cube-shaped houses lined up side-by-side. She estimated each one to be about twelve feet square so the entire block would be some forty-eight feet long. The line of the homes' long axis was at right angles to her path. She saw it first from the front. Each cube was outlined in black with a central door also outlined in black. Maintaining her distance from it as she walked, gradually she saw just the end of it. She did not want to disturb those cubes, and walked and breathed softly as she knew the people within them were asleep and must not be disturbed. Even as she walked forward, she had the very strong feeling she was going backward.

She went through a small alleyway and stopped when she came to the very edge of some water, her toes just touching it. It was shallow and as she looked far out over it, it seemed to continue forever. In the water, she saw a black track like a railroad track whose rails were about four feet apart and just reached to the water's surface. This passed directly in front of her and was so long she could not see its beginning nor its end either to her right or left. A single rail of the same size began at her feet and went out before her. It, too, seemingly went on forever.

The water was divided into squares about twelve feet on a side by some mechanism she did not understand. To her right was the only square that had ripples on it. They were perfectly symmetrical and in parallel rows with wavelets about one-half-inch high. All the waters of infinity were moving but they never left their squares. Nor did the squares coalesce or run into each other or lose their identity for these were living waters and their symmetries were etched in light. The water and concrete below it were absolutely level.

Very slowly did she loosen her mind from this dream. She wanted to understand all she could before letting the images slip back into the deeps. That afternoon she fell asleep reading St. John of the Cross and slipped immediately into the second dream.

She was walking up the stairs to the side of a large indoor pool with bleachers on the far side. She saw the right side of the pool was filled with silver bars and connected together like exercise equipment while the left side was perfectly empty and clear. Up and to her right a woman was standing in a cage such as announcers use. She talked continually. Her voice was dull and droning like any news commentator on a loudspeaker. June knew it was explaining about dolphins but she could not make out the words. It seemed to be speaking a different language and yet she was clearly receiving mental images. Suddenly, she was standing in the cool, clear water of that pool that came to her waist and she could no longer feel her legs or feet. It was a concrete pool and the sides were not more than twelve feet from her.

A dolphin swam by her left side, pressing, even

caressing her left hip. This feeling was delightful. It swung in front of her, close around her leg and stopped, looking at her as she looked at it. There was a kind of transparent cap covering the right side of its head. Perhaps, June thought, for some kind of experiment. The woman's voice said the hearing of dolphins is very good even with a cap on and June understood this particular bit of speech very well. The dolphin had a black back, gray sides and white underbelly. It rolled its head and looked at her out of its left eye.

"Maybe it wants the head cap removed." June worried about wires that might attach the cap; removal could hurt the animal. Again the dolphin looked at her and nuzzled against her thighs. June looked closely at the cap—it was held on by an elastic border. She put her fingers under the elastic and carefully removed the cap. The animal was not at all harmed and even seemed to be happy and relieved in its freedom. Then it swam past her left side, again caressing her hip. June turned to follow its course. It was now to her right and ahead of her, sitting on its tail like a dog with its head out of the water. It had come to look very much like a dog—smaller, black all over, and had a long nose like a German shepherd. It was listening intently to the woman's voice.

June found this very interesting, as she did not know dolphins sat like that. She petted it and caressed it and its skin was smooth and cool and firm. The woman was still talking but June did not look up at her. Her dolphin, her beautiful male dolphin, totally occupied her mind. It was obviously very happy about losing the cap and she thought of it as an exquisite and very nice animal.

"My, my, my, Mrs. Darnely, your dreams are always better than one could hope for. And this time I think the Angels of Dreams have outdone themselves. Shall we walk back through the first dream and put it in order in our minds?"

Light pinks chased themselves across her face under the pressure of his compliment. "Oh, yes. I'd love that."

"I have noticed that many dreams start with a crowd. Then the dreamer, just as you did, separates herself and the dream action begins. This again is a statement of the highly specific quality of the dream; it is meant for the dreamer only. You went into a hall to find your first husband and to test the waters, as they say. The questions that badgered your second marriage are resolved and now you wish to evaluate the first union because your commitment to it was total. Was there enough in that relationship to necessitate a change in the path you are now following? When Tibor turned the cheek of brotherly love instead of the lips of passion, you saw him in reality and realized he had no body. That is to say, he had no capacity for loving you as a wife. The man to your left; did you ever see him?"

"No, I have no idea what he even looked like."

"You understand what it means to stand to your left, but the enigmatic statement about the painting, that will net you all this money, may need a little embellishment. Money, of course, is gold and we have talked at length about that. The painting is any mental construct for all mental processes involve the transformation of images. When you have brought together the images of beauty, your life has evoked and put them into a form that can be appreciated by others—onto a canvas, into words, any medium that you choose—you have exchanged the gold of your intellect for the image of your creation. Therefore, you deserve to be compensated. 'The workman is worthy of his hire,' as our Bible suggests. You ask this man whom you never see to take you to your room."

He became silent and watched her for a moment. "Do you follow this? No? Listen, then. He vanishes and you are outside. Does that clarify what and where your room is?"

"Yes!" She said with dawning recognition. "Yes, I see! My room is infinity."

"Exactly, Mrs. Darnely, exactly. It is infinity and the proof is readily at hand. You see four cubical houses to your left joined in a line. The cube itself symbolizes the earth or earthy parts and four is the number of the intellect. The right angle that we use to form cubes is a gift from infinity. So, your four little houses are your intellect and it is sleeping!" His voice rose into his conclusive smile as he made this point but her slight frown showed it was not yet completely clear.

"You say my intellect was sleeping. In my dream I thought the people in those funny houses were sleeping."

"They are exactly the same. You are not your intellect but you can occupy it and then it is awake. Since it connects you to those about you, your dream may allude to it with equal validity as a plurality. Do you follow this? Excellent. So you tip-toe past the cubes and come to stand on the very edge of the great waters and there you find some things of the greatest interest. Not only are the waters shallow, but they are supported by flat concrete and they are separated into twelve foot squares. It is quite clear now that the eternal squares of infinity are the models that shape your cube houses. Which direction are you facing in that dream?"

"I suppose east. Don't we always face east?"

"Exactly. So the two rails are running north and south. You understand the train and its meaning so you may call these two rails the 'track of fate.' Your life is running on these at some point but you are also offered an alternate route. The single track that goes straight east is yours to use at any time. Would you like to summate these thoughts?"

"Yes. I found rejection from Tibor, found infinity to be my natural room, observed my own intellect sleeping as it must sleep if I am to see the Great Waters, and noted the tracks that my fate or I or both must follow."

"And you did not go into the waters."

"Correct."

"And now, Mrs. Darnely, the second dream—you do go into the waters. You are in the waters. You are in the waters up to your waist." He scratched his beard with his fingernail. "This is so reminiscent of the dialogue between the Buddha and the shepherd. Have you read that? No? It talks of the delight the shepherd knows when he experiences his wife in his bed and the Buddha answers of his delight when he experiences his soul in his bed. Your dolphin was certainly a physical treat for you and you felt him very clearly."

"Yes, yes, I am in the waters and the feeling of the dolphin on my skin was surely delightful. And, I did feel him very clearly. It must have been a dream of reality. I can surely understand how the Buddha must have felt." She sat forward on the edge of her seat and strained her mind toward him.

"Can we name him, animus? The male soul that swims in the deeps of your primal seas?"

She smiled. "I don't know what an animus is, but it seems like a good name."

"Agreed then. Now let us look at the next dream. The right side of this pool is filled with silver bars and exercise equipment. It is every bit as encumbered as your right or your physical side might be. The left side is calm and empty and inviting as your spiritual side is. The pool is in a concrete basin. Crete means calcium so you are in your own body and exercising your right mind. But, you are in the low point of your body and that explains your position in the pool. This is where the eternal waters flow. You are below your head and that is why you hear yourself from a cage giving the internal dialogue whose words you cannot decipher but whose message you understand at times and at times you hear the sound of the words only.

You hear yourself talking above you and from a distance, like through a loudspeaker, or at least the voice is that kind of hum-drum that you take to be from a speaker. The voice is going through REM sleep, and you hear the gibberish of memories clearing and the storage of things as one does in REM sleep.

"The dolphin has the cap on its right side. Cap-on is very close to capon and you know what happens to those poor birds. The dolphin's right side is not operant with the cap on. But when you remove the cap your soul can now hear and see what happens on both sides of your mind. It proves its new ability by sitting as a dog and listening to the woman talking. She is no other than you, mouthing your internal dialogue, which assures your sanity and under its control your soul sits on its tail like a dog. The dog is the turner, turning three times as it readies itself for sleep. It is descended from the wolf that guards the time of morning and evening when one can slip into the other world. Now, Mrs. Darnely, would you read Matthew 15:21-28?"

"I certainly will. 'And Jesus went thence, and departed into the coasts of Tyre and Sidon. And, behold, a woman of Canaan came out of the same coasts, and cried unto him, saying, Have mercy on me, O Lord, *thou* son of David; my daughter is grievously vexed with a devil. But he answered her not a word. And his disciples came and besought him, saying, Send her away; for she crieth after us. But he answered and said, I am not sent but unto the lost sheep of the house of Israel. Then came she and worshiped him, saying, Lord, help me. But he answered and said, It is not meet to take the children's bread, and to cast *it* to the dogs. And she said, Truth, Lord: yet the dogs eat of the crumbs which fall from their masters' table. Then Jesus answered and said unto her, O woman, great *is* thy faith: be it unto thee even as thou wilt. And her daughter was made whole from that very hour.'"

"Can you connect eating the crumbs from the masters' table to listening to the voice? Good. For they are quite similar and very important. But probably the most important fact of this dream is that the dolphin can turn in relation to you. You who have self-consciousness can also turn in relation to yourself. It is precisely this turning that gives you the ability to see yourself and seeing yourself means that you are conscious of yourself, or, self-conscious." His voice rose with the force of the argument.

"Or perhaps it is not the most important aspect of that dream. Consider what Jung experienced. In this dream, he was on a hiking trip along a little road through a hilly landscape. The sun was shining. He came to a small wayside chapel whose door was ajar so he walked in. A wonderful flower arrangement was displayed on the altar and in front of it was a yogi in the lotus position in deep meditation. He had Jung's face exactly. Jung said, 'I started in profound fright and awoke with the thought, so he is the one who is meditating me. He has a dream and I am it. I knew that when he awakened I would no longer be.'" He watched her face as she struggled to understand this.

"My, that is difficult. But," she shrugged. "I suppose you are telling me something. I probably don't want to hear it, though."

"We rarely do. What is the question, Mrs. Darnely?"

"The question, Dr. Zvee, is, who dreamed whom? Am I dreaming the dolphin or is the dolphin dreaming me?"

"Do you understand that, Mrs. Darnely? Do you really understand that?"

"No, frankly, I don't. But I fear I must accept it. Even worse, it's something I'll have to live with."

A long silence. "Well, Mrs. Darnely, what have you learned from all this?"

"I've learned a great deal about dreams and developed a deep respect for them. They are the diamonds of our existence. They are more important than we, or I anyway, ever imagined. As you said, 'To sleep because we must dream.' I see now that is the truth of it. Because we must listen for that dream voice that will guide us home; small wonder the Buddha has such large ears. If black holes connect one universe to another, then dreams are the black holes of our minds." She looked at him and shook her head slowly. "This is so odd, really. Here we are discussing the deep essence of dreams as though we had done this together all of our lives. It was not long ago that I desperately wanted to visit with you, and now I have and I have learned so much. And it still seems strange. So very, very strange."

"Yes, Mrs. Darnely, truth is stranger than fiction. But this is simply because life is choreographed by an infinitely creative mind of planning. This mind arranges and prepares and executes, and the most unlikely meetings and happenings come about with the precision of well oiled celestial mechanics. All to further a grand plan that sways the life of the earth in a diamond jaw grip. It was difficult for you, but we took enough time to develop the most hidden facts and subtle logic and I suspect its grandeur is now as palatable for you as chocolate truffles."

"My time has been extremely well spent. I have learned so much."

"And you have learned well. I wish you a long life and many more such dreams." He sat and looked fixedly into the wall for some time.

"Mrs. Darnely, it is sad to tell you this for I have enjoyed our dream sessions immensely but I will no longer be here for you. I have lived out the allotted Jacobean span and time has turned its enmity upon me."

"Dr. Zvee!" she gasped. "What are you saying?"

"Do not ask where I go nor what is for me. I will

work that out in my time. For you there is the preparing of yourself. For know that you must stand naked and alone before your God and one day bear His inquisitions. At that moment will all your knowledge and all your wisdom and all your goodness come to aid and defend you. Good fortune to you and may God look upon you with favor."

They walked slowly to the door together and they shook hands. He covered both of her hands in his and she his in hers. A long, long moment she looked into his eyes and saw that he too was deep in sadness. However, he could carry a great sadness as he had a great strength in his soul.

The dreams and quotes from Dr. Jung were taken from *Man and His Symbols* by Carl G. Jung or from *The Autobiography* of C.G. Jung.